Additional Acclaim for *One Foot in Eden*

"Rash's story is written with the crisp precision and evocative images you'd expect from a talented poet, especially one with deep roots in the region. His characters are vivid, thoroughly human. And his narrative unfolds in mesmerizing fashion . . . a page-turner with a palpable, moving sense of time and place, and an abiding compassion for the troubled humans who move through its pages."

—*The Charlotte Observer*

"A story of wild, almost primitive force and yet it is neatly and ingeniously put together. Ron Rash knows to the core the ways of those who yearn for what is just beyond their grasp. Here is a lasting experience."

—Fred Chappell, author of
Brighten the Corner Where You Are

"Ron Rash writes like a landscape painter. . . . Atmosphere and place are real—we are pulled right into that county and into the characters' minds. . . . Finally, it's a rich and lyrical language that is Ron Rash's gift to us, from the wise and moving words of the people in his novel to the whispers and secrets given up by the land he knows so well."

—*Creative Loafing*

"Ron Rash has written a hauntingly beautiful novel of a lost place and time, full of characters who have faced the truth themselves."

—Ashley Warlick, author of
The Distance from the Heart of Things

Also by Ron Rash

NOVELS

Saints at the River

The World Made Straight

SHORT FICTION

The Night the New Jesus Fell to Earth

Casualties

Chemistry and Other Stories

POETRY

Eureka Mill

Among the Believers

Raising the Dead

FOR CHILDREN

The Shark's Tooth

One Foot in Eden

a novel by

Ron Rash

PICADOR
HENRY HOLT AND COMPANY
NEW YORK

The author would like to thank Marlin Barton, Frye Gaillard, Tom Rash, Amy Rogers, and Robert West for their valuable assistance in the completion of this book.

www.picadorusa.com

Picador® is a U.S. registered trademark and is used by Henry Holt and Company under license from Pan Books Limited.

For information on Picador Reading Group Guides, as well as ordering, please contact the Trade Marketing department at St. Martin's Press.
Phone: 1-800-221-7945 extension 763
Fax: 212-677-7456
E-mail: trademarketing@stmartins.com

Book design by Leslie B. Rindoks

Library of Congress Cataloging-in-Publication Data

Rash, Ron, 1953–
One foot in Eden / by Ron Rash.
p. cm.
ISBN 0-312-42305-5
1. Dams—Design and construction—Fiction. 2. Appalachian Region, Southern—Fiction. 3. Real estate development—Fiction. 4. Relocation (Housing)—Fiction. 5. Loss (Psychology)—Fiction. 6. Mountain life—Fiction. I. Title.

PS3568.A698 O64 2002
813'.54—dc21 2002006677

First published in the United States by Novello Festival Press

10

For Bill Koon

One foot in Eden still, I stand
And look across the other land.
The world's great day is growing late,
Yet strange these fields that we have planted
So long with crops of love and hate.

—Edwin Muir

the
HIGH SHERIFF

THERE had been trouble in the upper part of the county at a honky-tonk called The Borderline, and Bobby had come by the house because he didn't want to go up there alone. I couldn't blame him. One badge, especially a deputy's badge, might not be enough. It was a rough clientele, young bucks from Salem and Jocassee mixed with young bucks come down from North Carolina. That was usually the trouble, North Carolina boys fighting South Carolina boys.

I had a good book on the Cherokee Indians I'd just started, but when Bobby knocked on the door I knew I wouldn't be reading any more this night. "Go have you a smoke on the porch," I told Bobby. "It'll take me a minute to get dressed."

Janice didn't open her eyes when I went into the bedroom to get my shoes and uniform. The lamp was still on, a book titled *History of Charleston* beside her. I looked at Janice, the high cheekbones and full lips, the rise of her breasts under the nightgown, and despite everything that had happened, and hadn't happened in our marriage, desire stirred in me like a bad habit I couldn't get shed of. I turned off the lamp.

Bobby and I followed the two-lane blacktop into the mountains. No light shone from the few farmhouse windows, not even a hangnail moon above. Darkness pressed against the car windows, deep and silent, and I couldn't help but think I was seeing into the future when much of this land would be buried deep underwater.

"It's a lonesome-feeling night, Sheriff," Bobby said, like he'd read my mind.

Bobby lit a Chesterfield, his face flaring visible for a moment before sinking back into the dark.

"Haints are bad to stir on a night like this," Bobby said, "leastways that's what my momma always claimed."

"So there are more things in heaven and earth than we might dream of?"

"What?" Bobby said.

"Haints. You believe in them?"

"I never said I did. I'm just saying what it was Momma notioned."

The fighting was over by the time Bobby and I had got to The Borderline. Casualties were propped up in chairs, though a few still lay amidst shattered beer bottles, cigarette butts, blood, and teeth. It was as close to war as I'd seen since the Pacific. I let them see my badge. Then I stepped through the battlefield to the bar.

"How'd this start?" I asked Bennie Lusk.

Bennie held a mop in his hands, waiting for the last men on the floor to get moved so he could mop up the beer and blood.

"How do you think?" Bennie said.

He nodded toward the corner where Holland Winchester sprawled in a chair like a boxer resting between rounds, a boxer in a fight with Jersey Joe or Marciano. Holland's nose swerved toward his cheek, and a slit in the middle of his forehead opened like a third eye. His clenched fists lay on the table, bruised and puffy. He wore his uniform, and if you hadn't known Holland was sitting in a South Carolina honky-tonk, hadn't seen the Falstaff and Carling Black Label signs glowing on the walls, your next guess would have been he was still in Korea, waiting at a dressing station to be stitched and bandaged.

"What do you reckon the damage?" I asked Bennie.

"Ten ought to cover it."

Bobby and I walked over to Holland.

"Sheriff," he said, his wrecked face looking up at me. "Looks like you got here too late to join the ruckus."

"Looks that way," I said. "But it seems you got your share of it."

"Yeah," Holland said. "Sometimes when a man's hurting on the inside a good bar fight can help him feel some better."

"I don't quite catch your meaning," I said. "All I know is you've caused a good bit of damage to Mr. Lusk's establishment."

"I reckon I did," Holland said, looking around as if he hadn't noticed.

"I know what it's like when you get back from a war," I said. "You need some time to settle back in. You pay Mr. Lusk ten dollars, and we'll leave it at that."

"I ain't got no problem with that, Sheriff," Holland said.

"Next time you'll go to jail," I said. I smiled but I leveled my eyes on his to let him know I was serious.

"We'll see about that," Holland said. He smiled too but his dark-brown eyes had gone flat and cold as mine.

He reached into his pocket and lay a leather pouch and roll of bills on the table.

"There, Deputy," Holland said to Bobby, peeling off a five-dollar bill and five ones. "You run that money over to Bennie."

Bobby's face reddened.

"I don't take my damn orders from you," Bobby said.

For a moment I was tempted to go ahead and cuff him, because it was sure as dust in August that we'd have another run-in with Holland and he wouldn't come quietly. Tonight he was already wore out and wounded. Tonight might be easy as it got.

"Take the money to Bennie," I said.

Bobby didn't like it, but he picked up the money.

Holland stuffed the roll of bills back in his pocket.

"Look here, Sheriff."

Holland opened the leather pouch and shook the pouch's contents onto the table. A Gold Star fell out, then other things.

"Know what they are?" Holland asked, dropping the Gold Star back in the pouch.

I stared at what looked like eight dried-up figs. I knew what they were because I'd seen such things before in the Pacific.

"Yes," I told Holland. "I know what they are."

Holland nodded.

"That's right, Sheriff. You would know. You was in the World War."

Holland held one up to me.

"You reckon them ears can still hear?"

"No," I said.

"You sure about that."

"Yes," I said. "The dead don't hear and they don't speak."

"What do they do, Sheriff?"

"They just disappear."

Holland placed the ear with the others. They lay on the table between us like something wagered in a poker game.

"There was some said it was awful to cut the ear off a dead man," Holland said. "The way I see it, taking his life was a thousand times worse and I got medals for that."

Holland picked the ears up one at a time and placed them in the pouch.

"These here won't let me forget what I did over there. I don't take it lightly killing a man but I ain't afraid to own up to it either. All I did was what they sent me there to do."

Holland stuffed the pouch into his pocket.

"What did you bring back, Sheriff?" Holland asked.

"A sword and a rifle," I said. "Nothing like what you got in that pouch."

Then Holland Winchester said the last words he would ever say to me.

"There's some that gets through it easier than others when the shooting starts, right, Sheriff?"

~

Those words were what I remembered two weeks later when Bobby interrupted my lunch.

"Holland Winchester's missing," Bobby said. "His momma's got it in her head he's been killed."

Bobby sounded hopeful.

"You don't think we'd be that lucky, do you?" I said.

"Probably not," Bobby said, the hope in his voice giving way to irritation. "Holland's truck is at the farm. It ain't like he would walk to a honky-tonk from there. He's probably just laying off drunk somewheres. Probably down at the river. I told her to call if he comes back."

"Let's give him a couple of hours to wander back home," I said. "Then I'll go up there and have a look-see."

Janice sat at the kitchen table, and she flinched when I said "look-see." Hillbilly talk, Janice called such words, but it was the way most folks still spoke in Oconee County. It put people more at ease when you talked like them, and when you are the high sheriff you spend a lot of time trying to put people at ease.

Janice wore a dark-blue skirt and white blouse. She had another meeting this afternoon. Friends of the Library, DAR—something like that.

"There's a missing person up at Jocassee," I said, "so I might not be back for supper."

"That will be fine," Janice said, not looking up from the table. "I won't be here anyway. Franny Anderson invited me to have dinner with her after our meeting."

I leaned over to kiss her.

"Don't," she said. "You'll smear my lipstick."

I walked back to the office and waited for Holland's mother to telephone. When no call came, I got in my patrol car and headed up Highway 288 toward Jocassee, toward what had once been home. The radio said it was over one hundred degrees downstate in Columbia. Dog days are biting us hard, the announcer said. I had the window down, but the back of my uniform already stuck to my skin as I left the town limits. The road was wavy with heat and humidity, its edges cluttered with campaign signs staked in the ground like tomato plants, some for General Eisenhower or Adlai Stevenson and even one for Strom Thurmond. Most were more local, including a couple with my name on them.

The blacktop steepened and pressure built in my ears until I opened my jaws. The road curved around Stumphouse Mountain, and beyond the silver-painted guard posts the land dropped away like those old European maps of the unknown world. If it were late fall or winter I would have been able to see a white rope of water on the far side of the gorge, a waterfall that had claimed two lives in the last twenty years.

The road leveled out, and suddenly I was in the mountains. It surprised me, as it somehow always did, that so much could change in just a few miles. It was still hot, but the humidity had been rinsed from the air. Pines got scarce, replaced by ash and oak. The soil was different too, no longer red but black. Rockier as well, harder to make a living from.

Dead blacksnakes draped on the fences told me what I already knew from the way corn and tobacco wilted in the fields—it had rained no more up here than it had in Seneca. I wondered how Daddy and my brother's crops were doing, and I reckoned no better.

I pulled off the road when I came to Roy Whitmire's store, parking beside the sign that said LAST CHANCE FOR GAS TWENTY MILES. I stepped past men sitting on Cheerwine and Double Cola crates. With their bald heads and wrinkled necks they looked like mud turtles sunning on stumps. The men gave me familiar nods, but the dog days had sapped the talk out of them. I swirled my hand in the drink cooler on the porch, ice and water numbing my fingers before I found a six-ounce bottle. I wasn't thirsty, but it wasn't right not to buy something. I stepped inside, into a big room that was darker than outside but no cooler.

The store was pretty much the way it had always been, the front shelf filled with everything from Eagle Claw fish hooks to Goody headache powders, a big jar on the counter, pickled eggs in the murky brine pressed against the glass like huge eyeballs. Next to the cash register another jar, this one filled with black licorice whips.

"Howdy, stranger," Roy said, grinning as he stepped from around the counter to shake my hand.

We made small talk a few minutes. My eyes adjusted to the dark and I saw the stuffed bobcat on the back wall—paw poised to strike, yellow eyes glaring—still at bay after three decades. Fifty-pound sacks of Dekalb corn seed lay stacked on the floor below it.

"I don't reckon you've seen Holland Winchester the last couple of days?" I finally said, getting to the reason I'd stopped.

"No," Roy said. "Of course I ain't exactly been out searching for him. I got enough trouble that's already found me without looking for more."

Roy lifted the nickel I'd placed on the counter, leaving the penny where it lay.

"Buffalo head," he said, holding the nickel between us. "You don't see many of them anymore. They done got near scarce as real buffalo. You sure you don't want to keep it?"

"No," I said.

Roy closed the register.

"Your daddy and brother, they're seeing a hard time of it, like most everybody with something in the ground. That ain't no good news for them or me."

Roy nodded toward the shelf behind him.

"I got a shoebox full of credit tickets. If it don't come a good rain soon I'd just as well use them to start my fires this winter. But you don't have to worry about such things down in town, do you?"

"No, I guess not."

I lay the Coke bottle on the counter.

"You telephone me if Holland comes by."

"I'll do it," Roy said. "You bring me one of your voting posters next time you're up this way. I'll put it in the window."

Before I got in my car I glanced at the sky. Like it mattered to me, a man with a certain paycheck come rain or drought.

A mile from the North Carolina line I turned off the blacktop and headed into the valley called Jocassee. The word meant "valley of the lost" to the Cherokee, for a princess named Jocassee had once drowned herself here and her body had never been found. The road I followed had once been a trail, a trail De Soto had followed four hundred years ago when he'd searched these mountains for gold. De Soto and his men had found no riches and believed the land worthless for raising corn. Two centuries after De Soto, the Frenchman Michaux would find something here rarer than gold, a flower that existed nowhere else in the world.

I took another right and passed fields where men once hid

horses during what folks up here still spoke of as the Confederate War. A war most folks in Jocassee had tried to stay out of, believing it was the slave owners' war, not theirs. When they'd been forced to choose, many had fought with the Union instead of the Confederacy, including several of my ancestors. Though I'd tried, there weren't enough votes in Jocassee to get the county to pave the road or even dump a few truckloads of gravel. Like almost everything else up here, the road was little different than it had been in the 1860s. But change was coming, a change big enough to swallow this whole valley.

On the road's left side was the land Carolina Power had bought from the timber company last winter, a thousand acres that ran all the way down to the Horsepasture River. The power company already had holdings on the other side of the water, and I doubted there was anyone left up here who didn't now know what Carolina Power was going to do to this valley.

It wasn't hard to figure out. All you had to do was look downstate at Santee-Cooper Reservoir. People up here wouldn't like it worth a damn to be run off their land, but when the time came there would be nothing they could do about it.

The road curved and dipped deeper into the valley. I passed my brother Travis's house and then the house I'd grown up in. Daddy worked in the far field, the dust plumes rising behind his tractor telling the whole story of the kind of year it looked to be.

The land leveled out. I smelled the river, but the road swerved left before I saw water. Branches slapped my windshield as I bumped over a road now no better than a logger's skid trail. I stopped at the battered mailbox with WINCHESTER painted on its side. I turned in and parked behind a blue Ford truck new as the telephone line that ran out of the woods. Holland was right. He'd done his portion of the killing Uncle Sam had sent him to do. A truck and telephone had been part of his reward.

Mrs. Winchester sat on her front porch. I knew she'd been

there a while, waiting for Holland or me to show up. I took off my hat and stepped onto the porch. I remembered seeing her when I was a boy and thinking how pretty she'd been with her long, black hair, her eyes dark as mahogany wood. She couldn't be more than fifty-two or three, but her hair was gray as squirrel fur now, her face furrowed like an overworked field. Only her eyes looked the same, deep brown like her son's.

Those eyes didn't blink when she spoke. Except for her mouth, her face was so rigid it could have been on a daguerreotype.

"He's dead," Mrs. Winchester said. "My boy is dead."

There was such finality in her voice I expected her to get up and lead me to Holland's body.

"How do you know that?" I asked when she didn't say or do anything else.

"I heard the shot. I didn't think nothing of it at first but when Holland didn't come in for his noon-dinner I knew it certain as I'm sitting on this here porch."

Her face didn't change, but for the first time grief and anger tinged her voice.

"Billy Holcombe's done killed my boy."

"Why would Billy Holcombe want to do such a thing?"

She didn't answer that question, didn't even try to. Ten years of experience told me there was more *wouldn't* answer than *couldn't* answer in her silence.

I looked at some corn planted close to the house. A scarecrow leaned like a drunk above the puny stalks. The hat and straw that had shaped the seed-sack face lay on the ground. It didn't matter. The drought had already taken anything the crows would want.

"When's the last time you seen Holland?" I asked, meeting her eyes again.

"This morning. I went out to feed the chickens. I come back and he was gone."

"And nobody came and picked him up?"

"No, I'd a heard it if they'd of done so."

"And Holland didn't say he was off to anywhere?"

"You go see Billy Holcombe," Mrs. Winchester said. "He's the one knows where Holland is."

Her eyes were stern and righteous, but I knew she wasn't telling me everything. For a moment I wondered if maybe she had done something to Holland, but that didn't seem likely. Everything I'd learned as a law man told me a mother who'd killed her grown child would have already confessed. She could have no more carried that burden inside her than I could have carried a baby inside me. What seemed likely was what Bobby had said. Holland was passed out somewhere drunk, someplace pretty close by since he hadn't taken his truck.

"I know the Holcombes is some kin to you," Mrs. Winchester said, and she let that hang in the air between us.

"If he's went and done something against the law that'll make no difference," I said, slipping more and more into the way of speaking I'd grown up with.

I put my hat back on.

"I'm going to have me a look around. I'll walk the river a ways and I'll go see Billy Holcombe, but I ain't accusing nobody of nothing yet. If Holland hasn't showed by morning I'll get a serious search going."

"He ain't coming back," Mrs. Winchester said.

She got up from the chair and went inside.

I walked down to a river that drought had made more dry stones than water. A current that would have knocked a man down in April was now a trickle. I limped across the shore of rocks as I followed the river downstream. I shouted Holland's name every so often, using what wind I had in my one good lung. But even if he wasn't passed out drunk, he'd have a hard time hearing me. Cicadas filled the trees, loud and unceasing as a cotton mill's weave room.

I straddled a barbed wire fence and stepped onto Billy Holcombe's land, land Billy had bought years back from Mrs. Winchester's husband. I wondered if that had something to do with why I was up here—an argument over a boundary line. Plenty of blood had been spilled over such matters in Oconee County. But I was getting way ahead of myself. I didn't even have a body yet.

Billy's tobacco pressed up close to the river. His rows were tight, no more than two feet apart, which meant more yield but the cultivating had to be done by hand. It was a good crop, bright green and tall, nothing like the tobacco in the fields I'd seen earlier. The river had saved him, soaking the soil so well in spring the roots still got moisture. Come fall he might be one of the few farmers in Jocassee with anything to cure in a tobacco barn.

Billy Holcombe hoed at the opposite end of the row where I stood, Cousin Billy, though a good ways back. He was a good bit younger than me, so I hadn't known him growing up, but I'd known his parents and older sister. All I remembered of him was that the first year I'd been down at Clemson College he'd gotten polio.

His being the only person in Jocassee to get polio hadn't been surprising, at least to the Holcombes' neighbors. Bad luck followed his people like some mangy hound they couldn't run off. His granddaddy and uncle had both owned farms at one time but lost them and ended up sharecropping for the Winchesters. They hadn't been trifling men. They'd worked hard and didn't drink, but it seemed the hail always fell hardest on the Holcombes' crops. If lightning hit a barn in Jocassee or blackleg killed a cow, it most always belonged to a Holcombe.

Billy's back was to me. The cicadas sang so loud he probably hadn't heard me calling Holland's name. I waited for him to finish his row, remembering how it felt to hoe tobacco—how the sweat stung your eyes and your back stayed bent so long you felt by day's end you'd need a crowbar to straighten yourself. I remembered how palms got rough as sandpaper and the back of your neck got red as brick and you'd get to the end of one row and keep your head down like a mule wearing blinders because you didn't want to see how many more of those long rows you had left.

But that wasn't the worst of it. The worst was knowing no matter how hard you worked, it might come to nothing. Even if the weather spared your crop, and that was a big if, you still had root knot and blue mold to worry about, not to mention bud worms and tobacco worms. Billy's tobacco looked healthy, but even so he wasn't home free yet. The hardest work came at harvest time. The tobacco gum turned your hands and arms brown as it stuck to your skin like pine resin. You had to string the leaves onto tobacco sticks and hang the sticks in the barn to cure. Even then a lightning strike or cigarette could set the barn on fire, and in five minutes nine months' work would be nothing but smoke and ashes.

Billy Holcombe knew all this better than I did, because it wasn't memory for him. It was as much a part of Billy as his own shadow. But as I watched him finish his row I knew he couldn't allow himself to think about how uncertain his livelihood was. To farm a man did have to act like a mule—keep his eyes and thoughts on the ground straight in front of him. If he didn't he couldn't keep coming out to his fields day after day.

I walked into the field, stepping on clumps of dirt and weeds Billy's hoe had turned up. That hoe rose and fell ahead of me, and despite myself it was like the hoe was in my hands, not his. For a few moments I could feel the worn oak handle smooth against my palms, could feel the hoe blade break the soil. Don't pretend you miss such a life as this, I told myself.

I didn't speak until he'd finished his row. He turned and found me not five feet behind him. For the first time I wondered if Mrs. Winchester might have spoken the gospel truth, because Billy didn't act at all surprised to see me.

"How you doing, Sheriff?" he said, meeting my eyes.

He didn't say *What's the matter?* or *Has something happened?* He spoke as if we'd just bumped into each other in downtown Seneca, not the middle of his tobacco field.

"I'm looking for Holland Winchester," I said, watching his blue eyes. "You seen him?"

"No," Billy said.

The eyes can lie, but eventually they'll tell you the truth. When Billy said no he glanced at his clenched right hand. I knew what that meant because I'd seen many another man do the same thing in such a situation. That right hand of Billy's had helped lift rocks from his field big as watermelons. It had helped fell oak trees you couldn't get your arms around. And maybe, just maybe, that hand had helped hold a shotgun steady enough to kill a man.

Billy Holcombe was looking for strength.

But I wasn't going to press him, not yet.

"Well if you do see him," I said, "tell him he's got his momma worried."

"I'll do that, Sheriff."

Billy wiped his brow with the back of his hand. He was sweating from the hoeing, but I wondered if he had another reason to sweat.

~

"If he doesn't come home tonight I'll bring some men with me in the morning," I told Mrs. Winchester. "We'll search the woods and river, if we need to."

I wrote down my telephone number.

"Here," I said, handing it to her. "You call if Holland comes in tonight. I don't care if it's three in the morning."

I got in the patrol car and bumped down the dirt road. I

thought again about what Holland had said to me two weeks ago about some men being better able to stand things when the shooting starts. I knew he was talking about more than just not getting killed or maimed so bad you wished you'd been killed. Holland was talking about how some men weren't much bothered by the killing. I had been, and I carried with me the glazed eyes of every Japanese soldier I'd taken the life from on Guadalcanal. But I'd fought with men like Holland who seemed bred for fighting the same way gamecocks are. Their eyes lit up when the shooting started. They were utterly fearless, and you thanked God they were on your side instead of the other. Like Holland, they'd wanted souvenirs from their kills, mainly gold teeth carved out with Ka-Bar knives, leaving the mouths of dead Japanese gapped-toothed like jack-o'-lanterns.

As I slowed at the mailbox with ALEXANDER painted on it, I wondered if Billy Holcombe could kill a man. If Holland Winchester didn't show up by morning I was going to have to give that question some serious thought.

Travis's truck was parked beside Daddy's, and Travis himself was on the roof. He'd heard me drive up but kept hammering until he'd used the half dozen nails clenched in his mouth. Then he stepped down the ladder to where I waited. We'd been born less than two years apart, and though we were both gray-eyed and tall, I'd always been big-boned like Daddy, while Travis favored Momma. But Travis had filled out in the last few years. There was no mistaking we were brothers, at least on the outside.

"What brings you up here," he said, and not in a welcome way. "I know it ain't your family."

His saying that rankled me, mainly because of the truth in it.

"I've been looking for Holland Winchester."

"What's he done now?" Travis asked.

"Disappeared."

"And you're wanting to find him?"

"Not particularly, but that's my job."

"Well he ain't here, Sheriff."

I let the "Sheriff" comment pass. I didn't want this visit to end like the last one.

"I was going to take Daddy over to Salem for supper."

"He's done ate," Travis said. "There was a time you'd have known that."

"Where is he?"

"Mending fence in the far pasture."

Travis waved the hammer toward the roof.

"That's why I'm doing this now. Everybody but Daddy knows he's too old to be cat-walking a roof. If he was here he'd not let me get up there without him helping me."

Travis clamped his mouth shut like it was a spigot he'd let run longer than he meant to. He glanced at the roof. I knew he wanted to get back up there, away from me. A whippoorwill called from the white oak in the back yard, its cry mournful as a funeral dirge.

"How are Will and Carlton?" I asked.

"Come around once in a while and you'd know."

"I been meaning to," and soon as I spoke I knew my words to be the wrong thing to say.

"Been meaning to," Travis said, his words mocking mine.

He stared at me, the same way he'd stare at a stump in his field or anything else bothersome he'd just as soon not have to deal with.

"How long has it been since you seen them or Daddy? Five months? Six? You think if you buy Daddy a cafe meal that's some big thing?"

"I don't need this, Travis," I said.

"No, you don't," Travis said, twisting my meaning. "You ain't needed anything up here for a long time."

Travis raised his hammer. For a second I thought he might throw it at me.

I couldn't have blamed him if he'd tried. Once we'd been close in a way I'd never been with my other brother or sister.

"You boys are ever alike as to share the same shadow," Momma had said when we were growing up. She hadn't been just talking about how we favored one another in our looks. It was something deep inside us—the way we knew what each other was feeling or thinking, the way we didn't argue and fight like most brothers. We had never said it, but we'd always believed no matter who else came into our lives—wives, children—we would always be that close. Travis believed I'd betrayed that pact, and I knew he was right.

"I got to finish this roof," Travis said.

"Tell Daddy I came by," I said, getting back in the car.

I drove out of the valley, the sun sinking into the trees. By the time I got on the blacktop, twilight had turned the strange color it always does in August, a pink tinged with green and silver. That color had always made it seem like time had somehow leaked out of the world, past and present blending together. My mind skimmed across time like a water spider crossing a pool, all the way back to 1935 when I was eighteen and Clemson had just offered me a football scholarship.

"I want to do something to help you celebrate," Janice Griffen had told me as we left homeroom. "How about dinner, at my house? My father will grill us steaks."

I had been too flustered to say anything but yes. Not only flustered but surprised by the invitation. Janice was a town kid, a doctor's daughter.

I had parked our family's twelve-year-old truck a quarter mile from Doctor Griffen's house. I wore my church clothes, my dress shoes blistering my heels as I walked past big white houses with front yards green as new money.

Doctor Griffen had met me at the door. He'd placed his arm around my shoulder and led me down a hallway wide as the road that led to my family's house, a burgundy-colored rug cushioning my steps.

I followed Doctor Griffen to a den lined with bookshelves. A mahogany writing desk filled one corner, a radio big as a pot-belly stove in the other.

"Have a seat," Doctor Griffen said. "Janice will be down soon."

In a few minutes we gathered around a huge oak dining room table. What struck me at that moment was how everything in that house seemed solid as that table, solid enough to weather a Depression that had caused men once rich to wander the country begging for work and food.

But I had been wrong. Even at that moment the house, the carpet and furniture, the very chair I sat in, was an illusion. Almost all of Doctor Griffen's money had been lost years before in the stock crash of 1929, the rest five years later in a land deal.

"Try your steak, Will," Doctor Griffen said after the prayer. "If it's too rare I'll put it back on the grill."

He spoke in a light-hearted way, as if an undercooked steak was the biggest concern he had. He was doing all he could, as he would the next three years, to keep an illusion alive for his daughter and wife.

I picked up my knife, but two forks lay to the left of my plate. I hesitated.

"This one," Janice had said, handing me the larger fork of the two.

~

When I drove into Seneca streetlights were on, the movie house marquee as well. SINGING IN THE RAIN COMING SOON, red letters claimed. There were plenty of farmers praying that marquee was right. The air seemed heavier, as it always did after I'd been in the mountains. I parked the car in front of the courthouse and walked across the street to McSwain's Cafe.

Darrell McSwain sweated like Satan's own cook as he flipped the liver mush and hamburgers sizzling on his grill. A fan blew right on him, but all it did was keep the smoke out of his face. Couples filled the booths. I nodded at the folks I knew and sat down on a stool. The jukebox played Lefty Frizzell's "Too Few Kisses Too Late."

"So what will you have, Sheriff?" Darrell asked.

"How about some cool weather?"

"Sold all I had to a drummer. Last I seen of him he was high-footing it to the Yukon."

"Then how about some ice tea and a burger."

"I can manage that," Darrell said, and turned toward his grill.

Someone had left a Greenville News on the counter. The Air Force was bombing the hell out of North Korea. Batista had more problems in Cuba. But these events seemed somehow farther away than when I'd read about them this morning. It was as if being in Jocassee had taken me out of the here and now.

"How are they going to do this year?" Darrell McSwain asked when he lay my supper on the counter.

I'd played football three years at Clemson, so Darrell and a lot of other people assumed I had some kind of lifelong loyalty. They seemed to forget what had happened after the spring game my junior year. I'd tore up my knee in that game, and Clemson had found a loophole to take my scholarship away.

"We'll make sure he gets his degree," Coach Barkley had promised Daddy when he recruited me, and that had been important to Daddy and especially my Uncle Thomas, who had the most education of anyone in Jocassee.

"There's nothing more valuable than what is behind this glass," Uncle Thomas had once told me, opening a child-tall bookshelf and handing me a book. "Knowledge is the one thing no one can take away from you."

I'd done my part, good grades in high school and at Clemson, but one hit on the knee and suddenly good grades and a promise made three years earlier no longer mattered.

"I haven't been keeping up with them, Darrell," I said, and he moved on down the counter with his tea pitcher.

I walked over to the office afterward. Mrs. Winchester hadn't called. I told Bobby to go home and get a good night's sleep, because it looked like we might be traipsing through woods and water come morning.

After a while I went home too, or at least what I called home now. Janice was in bed reading her book on Charleston.

"How was your meeting?" I asked.

"Frustrating, as usual. Gladys Williams had her silly suggestions. Anne Lester wouldn't agree to anything."

"I'm sorry to hear that," I said.

I undressed and got into bed. In a few minutes Janice lay the book on the table and turned off the lamp. The window was open, but no breeze fluttered the curtains. It was a night when sleep would come slow and fitfully, a night I would stare at a ceiling I could not see and think about the choices I'd made in my life, the choices my brother had reminded me of.

I pressed my chest against Janice's back, my hand rubbing her hip.

"No," she said, moving away.

The heat lay over me thick and still as a quilt. The only thing stirring was my mind, remembering that first year Janice and I had been married, remembering the nights Janice reached out for me. She would go to bed first because I'd be up to midnight doing my school work, my body bruised and aching from the afternoon's practice. The lights would be off, and I would undress and lie down beside her. Janice would pull me to her, no nightgown or slip, only her warm skin smooth against mine. I would be exhausted and she half asleep, and somehow that made it better, as if our hearts had an energy that went beyond our bodies, like we'd stepped out of time into the sweet everlasting.

I finally got out of bed, walked into the living room and picked up *Red Carolinians*, the book I'd just begun when Bobby had interrupted me that night two weeks ago. The story was one I'd heard about and seen parts of growing up in Jocassee, a story of people living and working land for generations and then vanishing, leaving behind the arrowheads and pieces of pottery I'd turned up while plowing. Leaving behind place names too—Jocassee, Oconee, Chattooga—each pretty, vowel-heavy word an echo of a lost world.

I thought of how the descendants of settlers from Scotland and Wales and Ireland and England—people poor and desperate enough to risk their lives to take that land, as the Cherokees had once taken it from other tribes—would soon vanish from Jocassee as well. Fifteen years, twenty at most, and it'll be all water, at least that was what the people who would know had told me. Reservoir, reservation, the two words sounded so alike. In a dictionary they would be on the same page.

There was a kind of justice in what would happen. But this time the disappearance would be total. There would be no names left, because Alexander Springs and Boone Creek and Robertson's Ford and Chapman's Bridge would all disappear. Every tombstone with Holcombe or Lusk or Alexander or Nicholson chiseled into it would vanish as well.

I looked at my watch. Past midnight and Mrs. Winchester still hadn't called. As I finished the book's last sentence, I wondered if Holland's body might also vanish under that coming water.

~

"The Bartram book hasn't come in yet, Sheriff," Mrs. Pipkin said the next morning. "I've unfortunately learned the employees at the state library are never in a hurry. A month ago my husband ordered a book he needed for his shop class. It still hasn't shown up."

Mrs. Pipkin slipped the library card into the book I'd returned, a book that had quoted Bartram. My Uncle Thomas had owned *Bartram's Travels*, and he'd let me borrow it when I was in high school. I wanted to read it again, so I'd asked Mrs. Pipkin to find a copy.

"Maybe it will come in today," Mrs. Pipkin said. "I'll let you know if it does."

Mrs. Pipkin disappeared into the fiction section to re-shelve a book.

Prim, that's how I supposed a novelist would describe Mrs. Pipkin—her hair tight in a bun, her spinster dresses and clipped, precise words. But she was attractive despite her best efforts. Her beauty was like a secret she couldn't conceal. I wondered if she lay down at night with her black hair loose about her shoulders. I wondered if there were nights she reached for the man who lay beside her, understanding that a woman's beauty is sometimes best revealed in darkness.

I walked across the square to the courthouse and telephoned Tom Watson and Leonard Roach while Bobby rounded up a dozen other men. Tom and Leonard rode with me, Leonard's bloodhound Stonewall lying between them on the back seat.

"You picked a good day to get us up in the hills, Sheriff," Tom said. "By noon-dinner time Seneca's going to be hot as a bellyful of wasps."

When we got to Mrs. Winchester's she met us on the porch.

"You'll be needful of this," she said, offering me what she clutched in a hand gnarled into a claw by rheumatism.

I took the shirt I hadn't had to ask for. She knew what we were about.

It was a grim business for her to see, Tom pulling the grappling hooks out of the back of the car in case we needed them, Leonard pressing Holland's shirt to Stonewall's nose as three carloads of men set themselves six feet apart to start their sweep through the woods.

Her expression didn't change as she watched though. She'd already buried a husband and two of her four children. It crossed my mind that a body to bury beside the others was all she hoped for now. I needed to know why she was so certain he was dead, so as Stonewall trotted through the woods toward Billy Holcombe's farm, I stepped up on the porch.

"I've got to know more than you've told me, Mrs. Winchester," I said. "I reckon you know that."

For a few seconds she didn't say or do anything. Then she nodded.

"So what can you tell me?"

"Holland was having relations with her," she said, not even blinking.

"You mean Billy Holcombe's wife?"

"Yes."

"And you heard a shot from over there?"

"I heard it," Mrs. Winchester said. "What Holland went and done wasn't right, but he shouldn't ought to have died for it."

Stonewall bayed closer and closer to Billy Holcombe's farm. What she told me was the truth, all of it, because it all made sense—Billy acting so unsurprised to see me, Holland disappearing but his truck being here, the shot she'd heard.

"He was wearing his soldier uniform," Mrs. Winchester said. "He always wore it when he went over there."

For the first time her voice wavered.

"However is it fair that he could do all that fighting in Korea and not get much more than a briar scratch, then come back home and get shot in his own back yard? Can you answer me that, Sheriff?"

I shook my head. I had no answer, at least none I wanted to

tell her. She was an old woman who'd outlived two, maybe three, of her children. Whatever mistakes she'd made raising them she didn't need to be reminded of. I just looked down at the ground between us, knowing she and I had more in common than she probably realized.

I had lost a child too, not like her but in my own way. There had been times as the years passed when I'd wonder what that child would have looked like had it been born alive. I'd imagine a child at five or six or eight or ever how many years had passed since the miscarriage. Sometimes I'd imagine a boy, sometimes a girl. Picking at scabs, that was all I was doing at such times, but I couldn't seem to stop myself.

I put my hat back on.

"I'll do all of what I can to find your son, Mrs. Winchester."

"I thank you for it," she said.

I stepped off the porch and walked into the woods, meeting Leonard and Bobby and Tom on their way back.

"It's like he's done disappeared into thin air, Sheriff," Leonard said. "We got out there in front of Holcombe's house and the trail went colder than grave frost. I figured I'd start Stonewall again out in front of Mrs. Winchester's, see if he can sniff up another trail."

"If Stonewall doesn't, you all start dragging the river," I said. "You speak to anybody over there?"

"No," Bobby said. "I saw Holcombe's wife peeking behind a window but she didn't come out."

"Well, I'm going to talk to the both of them. I'll get up with you later."

I walked on, the cicadas making their racket above me in the trees, calling for rain as Daddy used to say. Doing a pretty poor job of it too, for the pieces of sky I saw through the trees were blue as a jaybird.

I stepped through the barbed wire fence. Down toward the river I saw Billy in his field, but I stepped up on the porch instead. I rapped my knuckles on the door.

When she looked at me through the screen I saw what had brought Holland this way. Amy Holcombe was blue-eyed with yellow hair that fell to her waist, tall and slim but full-breasted. When she opened the screen door, I saw she was pregnant.

I wondered right then and there whose child it was.

"What brings you out this morning, Sheriff?" she asked, trying to act surprised—as if she hadn't noticed the dog and searchers tramping all over her yard.

"Holland Winchester's missing," I said. "His momma says he was over here yesterday."

"I don't know the least thing about that," Amy Holcombe said, and she said it in a flat kind of way, the way someone would say something they'd memorized for a test.

"You mind me visiting with you a minute, Mrs. Holcombe?" I asked and stepped a little closer.

"I've got a bushel of chores to do," she said. "I ain't even cleared breakfast off the table."

"Just for a minute, Mrs. Holcombe. Then I'll be on my way."

She didn't want to let me in, but I could tell she was calculating it would be more trouble not to. She opened the screen door wider.

"The house is ever a mess. Like I said, I got a lot to do."

I smelled the wood smoke as I stepped inside and remembered I hadn't seen a gap in the trees for a power line. A clock that didn't work lay on the mantle above the hearth. Beside it an oil lamp, against the wall a couple of ladder-back chairs. That was enough to know they were poor in a way none of my people had been since the Depression. They got water from a well, and they still used an outhouse. I wasn't even sure they had a truck. There'd been no tire tracks in the weeds and rocks that passed for a driveway.

She didn't ask me to sit down, but I did anyway.

"I can get you some tea to drink," she said, but her tone made it clear she didn't want to get me anything other than out of her house.

"No, thanks."

She sat down in the other chair.

"I just wanted to ask you about Holland Winchester. Like I said, his momma thinks you might know something."

"I didn't know," Amy Holcombe said, and she caught herself, because what she was going to say was either "I didn't know him" or "I didn't know him hardly at all." Either way it was past tense, the tense used to speak of the dead.

"I didn't know him to be missing," she finally said, and that was slick on her part because she didn't have to take back the *I didn't know*.

"I think maybe you and your husband know where he is," I said. "It's going to be easier on everybody if you all just go ahead and admit it."

"I don't know nothing about where Holland Winchester is," she said, getting up from her chair. "I got things to do, Sheriff."

"You won't mind me looking around, will you?"

"Me and Billy, we got nothing to hide," she said. She picked up the broom like she was going to sweep me out if I didn't move toward the door on my own.

I got up from the chair. Nothing to hide but a body, I thought, a body I believed would turn up soon enough.

"Goodbye, Mrs. Holcombe," I said, but she'd already turned her back to me.

The sunlight was bright and startling after being in the house. I checked the barn first and found a truck with two flat tires and a cracked engine block. The only way that truck could have moved was if there'd been a team of horses to drag it. That was good news for me. Holland's body couldn't be too far away. I stepped in the woodshed, and after that I peered down the well. I wasn't seriously searching, just getting a feel for the layout of the farm.

I watched Billy out in his field. He hadn't tried to make a run for it, the way many another man might have. Instead, he was going about his business. I wondered for the first time if I'd underestimated him. I wondered if he might be like those men I'd known in the Pacific, the ones you'd have expected to be the first to cut and run and then in battle they surprised you, surprised themselves.

I had been a man like that, though I was big and stout-looking enough to fool everybody but myself. I hadn't known what I would do in battle, and the morning I waited for the LAV to land on Guadalcanal, I was so afraid I threw up.

"The hillbilly's not used to the ocean," one of the other soldiers said, but it wasn't seasickness. Then we'd waded in, and I heard a thump against the chest of the man beside me. He stopped as if he'd forgotten something on the LAV as a stain blossomed on the front of his uniform. The sand puffed up in front of me from a bullet aimed too low, and I felt in that moment something of what I'd felt in football games after the first hit, the first smear of blood on my jersey. The fear was still there, but it was muted, like the sound of the crowd is once the game starts. Even my bad knee didn't seem to slow me down. I ran for the tree line like a wingback zig-zagging to avoid tacklers. I made it but was still gasping the watery tropical air when a Japanese soldier raised up ten yards in front of me. I aimed for his heart and I found it.

In the three weeks before a bullet pierced my lung and sent me back home, I'd killed at least three other men.

"I'm giving you this deputy's job because you know if it comes to the have-to you can kill a man," Sheriff McLeod had told me after I got back to Seneca.

"Yes sir," I'd answered, glad to have a job outside a mill, a job where I'd get to use my brain some, use it even more when Sheriff McLeod retired two years later.

As I walked down the field edge to where Billy worked, I started a conversation with myself, because there had been times doing such had helped me solve crimes. *O.K., Billy, where would you hide a body? Maybe in the barn loft? Maybe the bottom of the well? It doesn't seem likely. You had to know those were the kinds of places we'd look first. Maybe in the woods, but a fresh-dug grave would stick out like a No-Heller in a church full of Hardshell Baptists. Besides, the ground is hard as cement. No, Billy,* I said to myself. *You didn't bury that body.*

The season was against him. It was the time of year when the Dog Star rose with the sun, and while that meant hot weather and little rain, there was more to it than that. The old Romans had considered it an unwholesome season, and it was hard not to agree with them. Ponds and rivers got scummy and stagnant this time of year, the air still and heavy, like a weight pressing down. The cattle got pinkeye and blackleg, and a dog or cat could go mad. Polio got worse too, or so people believed. Children weren't allowed to go swimming or to picture shows.

For Billy it also meant a dead man would bloat and rot twice as fast. If he didn't bury Holland's body, anybody within a half mile would soon enough smell it.

Unless he put it in the river, and that was where I figured the body to be. Low as the river was it could still hide a body, especially if you weighted it down with a creek rock or waterlogged tree.

Billy saw me coming and raised up from topping his tobacco. He stood in the middle of a row. The first stick of dynamite went off and then another, but Billy didn't take his eyes off me. I thought for a moment he might raise his hands over his head and make it easy for all of us, but he didn't.

Then I saw them, drifting down slow as black ashes over the trees across the river. To tell the truth I was disappointed in Billy. He hadn't kept his head about him after all. It was almost funny the way he stood in the field facing me, doing his best to look innocent while right behind him the buzzards in the sky marked a giant X where Holland's body was. Billy's shotgun lay at the end of his row, and I stood between him and it.

"Looks to be something dead over yonder," I said.

I waited for Billy's face to go pale as he looked over his shoulder and saw he'd forgotten about buzzards when he'd hidden Holland's body. I'd seen men piss on themselves at such moments. Others would cry, or fall down, or run though they knew there was nowhere to run to, run like chickens that had just had their heads cut off and their bodies didn't yet know they were doomed.

"It's my plow horse," Billy said, hardly giving the buzzards a glance. "He broke his leg yesterday."

And that set me back, set me back hard as if he'd sucker-punched me in the stomach. He couldn't have come up with a lie that quick and delivered it that matter-of-fact, at least I didn't believe he could.

"That's some hard luck," I told him.

We talked a couple more minutes, but before I could bring up what Mrs. Winchester had told me and Bobby, Tom and Leonard sloshed out of the river, Stonewall loping behind them.

"Bring up anything?" I asked.

Tom opened his pack to show a big trout the dynamite had blown out of the water. I pointed out the buzzards to them.

"Damn," Bobby said. "I guess we been looking down when we should of been looking up."

"You want us to go look?" Tom asked, but I told them I'd take care of that, for them to go on to town for lunch, round up some more men if they could and get back by two o'clock. They started to leave, but I nodded at Bobby to stay a few moments longer.

"What you got the .12 gauge for?" I asked Billy.

"Groundhog been troubling my cabbage," he said, and that was a reasonable enough answer.

"You seen him lately?" I asked.

"Who?" Billy asked.

Smart, Billy, I thought, *but be careful you don't outsmart yourself.*

"The groundhog," I said.

"No, I don't expect I will with you all blasting up the river."

"Then you won't mind Bobby taking your shotgun with him. We might need to check it if a body turns up. Besides, I don't like to be around loaded guns. I'm bad superstitious that way."

"Suit yourself," Billy said, like it was no matter to him.

Bobby picked up the gun and left. I squatted down and wiped my glasses, something to do while I thought about what should come next.

Leonard and Stonewall had come up with nothing. Neither had the men searching the water and woods. We'd search the other side of the river come afternoon, and Tom could take his grappling hook and dynamite farther downstream. Surely Holland's body would show up by dusk.

But maybe I wouldn't have to wait that long, I thought. Maybe if I got under Billy Holcombe's skin he might save me a few hours.

"I'm going to give you the lay of the land, Billy," I said. "Then I'll let you have your say. Mrs. Winchester says Holland was tomcatting around with your Missus. She believes you done shot and killed him for it."

Come on, Billy, I thought. *Get riled up. Tell me what a worthless son of a bitch Holland was. I'll not argue with the truth of that. Tell me how he threatened you or your wife. Tell me how it was self-defense. Confess and we'll get this over with here and now.*

"That's all lies," Billy said, but the lack of heat in his voice argued otherwise.

"She claims she heard the shot."

"She heard me shoot my plow horse."

"She claims the shot was near your house," I said, not giving him much as a second between questions. "Maybe even inside it."

"She's a old woman. She's just addled."

"What about your wife and Holland?" I asked.

"That's a lie."

I looked at the buzzards. I'd have to walk over in a minute and make sure that was a horse they were drawn to. My knee wouldn't enjoy risking a slip in the river, but there was nothing to be done about that.

"So you wouldn't have a problem with me checking inside your house?"

"No," Billy said.

His face showed me little. He was getting more comfortable with his lies, like a card player learning how to bluff.

"Or anywhere else on your land."

"No."

"And you shot that horse yesterday morning as well?"

He caught what I was trying to do.

"I shot my horse yesterday morning, but I didn't shoot nothing else."

"So your horse broke its leg plowing?"

"Yes," Billy said. "I was plowing my cabbage and his hoof got slicked on a rock. I didn't want to smell him so I took him over the river, put him back a ways in the woods."

That made sense but only up to a point. *You may have gotten a bit too clever for your own good, Billy,* I thought.

What I said was, "Let's go have a look at that horse."

I let Billy lead, both of us taking our time as we made our way down the bank. He stepped into the water, but slow and careful, careful beyond worrying about slipping. He was scared, scared because it was clear he couldn't swim. *That would make it harder to sink a body deep where you'd want it, Billy,* I thought. *It could still be done, but you'd have a rougher time of it. Maybe that body is in the woods after all,* I told myself.

I stepped into the water right behind him, close enough to grab him if he slipped, if he tried to run when he got to the far bank. That would have been quite a spectacle, the two of us limping through the woods on our game legs, him trying to get away, me trying to catch up. But though I stayed close I really didn't believe he'd run. Yesterday, that would have been the time for that. It was too late now, too late for a lot of things.

A crime of passion, Billy, that was your defense, I thought as I followed him through the shallows. *You should have come into my office yesterday and turned yourself in, telling it all up front about Holland and your wife. You'd have probably gotten off light, Billy, even if it was a war hero you killed. But you've messed up now. You hid your crime. You made it seem calculated, premeditated.*

The water rose to my knees but no higher.

Press a one-inch piece of curved metal with your index finger and your world changes forever, doesn't it, Billy. Just a little thing like the pressing of a bit of metal, or a little thing like a teammate banging his shoulder pads into the side of your knee in a scrimmage—an accident, not even a hard hit, just a little popping sound inside your knee.

"My father will help us" was what Janice had said after Coach Barkley told me I no longer had a scholarship. I was married by then, Janice two months pregnant. What she meant was that her father would give us money to finish my teaching degree, money to help with the baby. But Janice had come back from her parents' house with the news her father was poor as any Jocassee farmer. I dropped out of school to work at Liberty Mill. Then came the miscarriage, and hospital bills made sure not even night classes were a possibility.

"Something's wrong," she'd said that June night.

I'd reached up and turned on the lamp. Blood soaked the bed's center, the blood of our child. We frantically pushed away from the sagging middle of the bed—away from each other. Away from the stain that widened between us.

"Severe tearing and scarring of the cervix," the doctor told Janice and me three days later as we'd prepared to leave the hospital. "I'm sure you know what this means."

Janice and I had a pretty good idea what it meant, but neither of us said a word, as if by not answering we might at least keep something alive.

"You won't be able to have children," the doctor said.

As I'd helped Janice out of her seat she winced in pain. I'd held onto her arm and we'd walked out of the hospital slow and careful, like people who no longer trusted even the ground beneath them.

~

I smelled death soon as Billy and I struggled up the bank, its odor stronger with each step deeper into the woods. Then I saw it. There were so many buzzards it was hard to tell at first what they huddled over. Every buzzard in Oconee County seemed to have gathered, the trees black with others waiting their turn. I held a handkerchief to my face and waded in among them. I kicked off enough to see Billy had told the truth about at least one thing.

"Let's get the hell out of here," I said.

We waded back across the river before I asked him the question that had made me think he might be lying about what was drawing the buzzards.

"How did you get a horse with a broke leg across a river?" I asked.

I could tell right away that question was one he hadn't expected. His eyes locked on his right hand, the same as they'd done the day before. Looking for strength. I bet he didn't even know he was doing it, but it was good as any lie detector machine.

"I beat hell out of him," he said, but a good ten seconds passed before he thought up that lie.

Billy turned his back to me and started topping his tobacco. I just stood there a minute. Letting him know I didn't need to rush off to look for any more suspects because we were past the suspect stage now.

When did it start to go wrong for you, Billy? I wondered. *Are you like me? Can you remember one thing—a harsh exchange of words, a bad harvest, a morning when she offered her cheek instead of her lips when you kissed her? I know when it went wrong for me,* I thought, *and here's the worst thing, Billy. I believe Janice and I would be different people now, better people. That miscarriage wouldn't have happened. We would have children, and I'd be a teacher, maybe at a college. At night Janice wouldn't turn her back to me, Billy. Something cold wouldn't have locked inside our hearts if I had been one step slower or quicker to that ball carrier, if the coach's whistle had stopped one play a second quicker.*

I left Billy in his tobacco field and walked through the woods to Mrs. Winchester's house. I told her we'd be back that afternoon. Then I headed up the dirt road to see Daddy.

He came out of the barn when I drove up. Daddy had aged a lot the last few years, especially since Momma had died. His heart gave him trouble, and the doctor had told him he needed to slow down. He had sold most of his cattle and worked fewer acres.

But Daddy still did more than he should. He wasn't a man who could sit on a porch all day or spend afternoons up at Roy Whitmire's gas station playing checkers and gossiping. I knew Travis would find him one day soon face down in a field or pasture. From what the doctor said it was a miracle it hadn't already happened.

"Travis said you was hunting for Holland. Found him yet?" Daddy asked.

"No sir, not yet. But we still got some woods and river to cover this afternoon."

"You been upriver to see the Widow?"

"Not yet."

"I reckon you'll have to," Daddy said.

"If nothing doesn't show by late afternoon I expect so."

"You ain't skittish to go up there, are you?"

"No sir."

"Good, for there's a many who are. People always have wanted to believe the worst things about her."

"She's done herself no favors shutting herself up in that hollow by herself," I said. "That's the kind of thing gets people to talking."

"If that suits her I see no reason for it to be anyone else's concerning," Daddy said.

He looked at his watch.

"You ate?"

"No sir. I was thinking you and me could go over to Salem and get a bite."

"No need for that," Daddy said. "Laura brought over some collards and peas the other evening. Fixed me a pone of cornbread too. We'll warm that up."

"I thought you might enjoy cafe food for a change."

"No," Daddy said. "What I got here fits me fine."

I knew if I went to Salem I'd be going by myself, so I went inside and sat at the kitchen table while he warmed the food. The kitchen looked like it always had in some ways—the Black Draught calendar above the stove, the metal tins of sugar and salt on the counter. But Momma's recipe box wasn't on that counter. There was no sifter or rolling pin out. The kitchen didn't have the warm smell it'd had when I was growing up and Momma always seemed to have bread or a pie in the stove.

Memory took me back to a winter evening when Travis and I had walked home after hunting squirrels on Sassafras Mountain. It had started snowing, flakes big as nickels swirling down from a low, gray sky. By the time we stepped out of the woods we couldn't see our feet, but we could see the yellow pane of light across the pasture. That glowing window was like a beacon leading us to a warm, safe place where people who loved us would always be waiting.

Maybe that's the best blessing childhood offers, I thought as Daddy lay my plate before me, believing that things never change.

"That's better than any cafe food," Daddy said.

There had been a time I would have agreed with him. The thick, salty tang of fatback added to the collards and field peas would have made it taste all the better. Laura's crackling cornbread would have tasted sweet and moist as cake. Now the food tasted greasy, sliding down my throat like motor oil.

"Country food," Janice called it. The few times we'd come up here for Sunday dinner and a bowl of collards or plate of venison had come to her she'd smiled and said, "No, thank you," and passed the bowl or plate to the next person.

"How's Janice?" Daddy asked, as he always did.

"She's just fine, Daddy."

"That's good to hear," he said.

I could hear the cicadas singing in the trees as we tried to think of something else to say. Though we sat five feet apart, it seemed a lake had spread out between us, but it was something wider and harder to get across.

"You need to see them twins," Daddy finally said. "They done growed up on us."

"I mean to do that, Daddy. If we don't find Holland this afternoon I'll try to go by there tomorrow."

"One of them boys carries your name, son," Daddy said, trying to make his tone gentle. "You shouldn't have to already be up here to let him catch sight of his uncle."

Daddy looked at his empty plate. There was nothing for me to say. Like Holland when he'd decided to get involved with another man's wife and Billy when he'd decided to do something about it, I'd made my choice.

"We could use some rain," Daddy said, trying to move us past what he'd said about my nephews. I knew he'd make small talk the rest of my visit. He would have said the same words to a stranger, and I wondered if that was what I had become to him, a stranger who had once been a son.

"Yes sir," I said and drank the last of my tea.

"You want some more?" he asked.

"No. I need to get back over to Billy Holcombe's farm."

"You think he had something to do with Holland disappearing?" Daddy asked.

"I think he killed Holland."

"I just can't notion Billy doing something such as that."

I got up from the table.

"People can disappoint you sometimes, Daddy. I reckon you know that well as anybody."

Daddy knew what I was saying.

"Come back when you can," he said.

I walked on out to the car. Daddy stood in the doorway and watched me back down the drive to the county road. As a young man he'd been a legendary hell-raiser, like Holland a man bad to drink and fight. After he'd married Momma he'd settled down, working dawn to dusk to make sure we had clothes and shoes and never went hungry. We never had, even in the leanest of times during the Depression. He'd held onto this land too, land that had been in his family for one hundred and eighty years.

He had held onto it not only for those who'd come before him but for his children and grandchildren. I knew his greatest satisfaction was being able to look in the fields and see his son and grandsons working the same land he'd worked all his life. He'd heard the talk about Carolina Power flooding the valley, but I knew he couldn't have believed there'd be a time when Alexanders didn't farm this land. I hoped he was dead before Carolina Power had the chance to take that belief from him.

He'd prepared Travis and me to carry on what Alexanders had done here for six generations. Daddy had been a stout, rough-looking man, a man not to be trifled with. But he'd taught us in a patient, caring way, his hand always light on our shoulders. When I went off to Clemson, he'd believed it was only for a few years, that I would come back to Jocassee.

Now he was an old man with a bad heart and a farm that would one day vanish completely as a dream. A man whose oldest son had become little more than a stranger. I stared through the windshield at his lean, craggy face like I'd watch something about to be swept away by a current, for I realized this could well be the last time I saw him alive.

Right then I decided I wouldn't run for re-election. I'd serve out my term and then come back here and live with him. I'd farm this land until Carolina Power ran us all out and drowned these fields and creeks and the river itself. However long that was, it would give me some time to be a son and a brother again, maybe even learn how to be an uncle.

I backed out of Daddy's driveway and headed toward Billy Holcombe's farm, but it was like the car was driving itself. My mind was busy mapping the future.

I'd ask Janice to come with me, but I knew she wouldn't. I'd pack up a few clothes and leave the savings and house and car. It sounded so easy, but it wouldn't be. I would carry fifteen years of being part of another person's life away with me as well. I wouldn't be able to shuck a marriage the way I could a house or job.

I checked my watch. One-thirty. Janice was probably at a tea or playing bridge. She'd be wearing a hat and hose despite the weather, still playing the role of the wealthy doctor's daughter.

"Where's Mrs. White Gloves?" a town councilman had asked his wife at a Christmas party when he didn't know we were behind him.

"Probably still at home teaching the sheriff the proper way to unfold a napkin," the councilman's wife had said.

You want to think the worst of her, I told myself as the road curved with the river. *It's easier than the truth—that sometimes what goes wrong between two people is nobody's fault.*

I remembered what else the councilman had said that night, what Janice had heard as clearly as I had.

"Thank God she and the sheriff don't have any children. Can you imagine what kind of mother she'd be?"

"Please don't," Janice said when she stopped me from grabbing the councilman by the collar. "Their snippy comments don't mean a thing."

But the hurt in Janice's eyes had argued otherwise.

~

By two o'clock, forty men had gathered in front of Billy Holcombe's house. Besides more dynamite, Tom Watson had brought another grappling hook and some bamboo poles to poke undercuts with. I gave him five more men and sent him on his way. Leonard led the rest across the river to search the Carolina Power land.

"Keep your noses and eyes open," I said as they walked away. "I know there's a dead horse over there. There might could be a dead man as well."

I turned to Bobby.

"Anything I need to know of back in town?"

"Mrs. Pipkin brought over a book, said it was the one you'd asked her to get from the state library. That's about it. It's too hot for people to get into much meanness."

"I reckon so."

I nodded toward Billy Holcombe's house.

"Let's go have us a look-see."

"We've come to search," I told Amy Holcombe when she came to the door.

She didn't say a word, just stepped out of our way. I went straight to the back room. I wasn't looking for a body. I was looking for a murder scene. Bobby and I stripped the sheets off the mattress, but there was no bloodstain and none on the floor. We checked the closet and under the house. There was no bloody sheet, no fresh-packed dirt. Bobby climbed into the well and poked the bottom with a hoe handle. Then we searched the barn and shed, but we knew soon as we stepped inside there was no body in either, because in the dog days there's no hiding the smell of death.

"I'm about convinced that son of a bitch is off somewheres still alive and having a good laugh at us," Bobby said.

"No," I said. "Holland's dead and he's within a mile of where we're standing."

"You're sure of that?" Bobby said.

"Yes," I said.

I needed to get inside Billy's head, a head that held a lot more smarts than I'd earlier imagined. I needed to think the way he did to figure out what had been done. That had worked in the past when I'd searched for a runaway from a chain gang or for a lost child or a whiskey still. Once you locked in on how a person saw the world, the hiding place could become no harder to find than a lightning bug on a July night. But that wasn't the only reason I wanted to live Billy's life awhile, sorry as it was. I was weary of living my own, glad to take my mind off a decision I was telling myself I'd already made.

"Get a couple of men and go check his fields," I told Bobby. "Maybe he's done some late planting this year."

"That's a good idea," Bobby said. "I'd not thought of that."

"Be careful not to trample his crops," I said.

I sat down on a chopping block outside the woodshed and looked out over the dying beans and corn to where Billy worked. I knew the why and the how, and I pretty much knew the where. Like I'd told Bobby, that body was within a mile of where I sat. There was no way it couldn't be. I knew the plow horse had hauled the body, because Holland was too big for Billy to carry.

Suddenly I realized something, not the answer but what would lead to the answer—the horse hadn't broke its leg in the field but while carrying Holland's body across the river. Its hoof had slipped on a slick rock, just like Billy had said, but that rock had been in the river. The weight on its back had done the rest.

What had happened then, Billy? I thought. *You probably did what you said. You beat the hell out of that horse and got it up the bank and into the woods and then shot it. But you got Holland's body off first. You left it there in the river or on the bank. You came back and tied a creek rock to the body and wedged it in an undercut or sank it deep in a pool. You didn't bury it in the ground, Billy. You were smart enough to know better. Your best chance was the river, your only real chance, because water can keep things covered up, even in a time of drought.*

I checked my watch. Almost five-thirty. I'd heard the dynamite blasts off and on for the last three hours, but Tom would have let me know if something had come up. The same with Leonard. I watched the men out in the field, moving slow through the tobacco as though wading through a pond. Billy worked out there among them, doing his best to act like he didn't even notice all the commotion around him.

"I know the Holcombes is some kin to you," Mrs. Winchester had said. I didn't want her or anyone else saying I hadn't done everything possible to find out what had happened to Holland. So there was one other thing to be done, a visit I'd put off long as I could.

She lived a good mile upriver. My scarred lung and knee begged me to send Bobby, for it was an up-and-down mile. But I knew how superstitious Bobby was. He'd grown up in Long Creek but had kin who'd lived in this valley, including his Uncle Luke who'd been the Widow's neighbor for a while. Bobby would know the stories about her. He'd no more make a visit to that old woman than he'd spend the night in a graveyard. No, I'd have to be the one to call on Widow Glendower.

I followed the river up past the old Chapman place to where Wolf Creek flowed into the river.

Once when Travis and I had been kids we'd fished Wolf Creek. It had been October, the time of year when brown trout swim into creeks to spawn. We'd started at the river where the creek entered and caught two trout right off, big males with hooked jaws, the spots on their sides big and bright as holly berries. Travis and I had worked our way on up the creek, dragging our heavy stringers behind us. One more pool and we'll turn back, we kept telling each other, because we knew who lived at the head of that creek. But the fishing was too good. We'd kept on going.

Then we came to where the creek forked. Between the two forks stood Widow Glendower, like she'd been expecting Travis and me. She was dressed in her black widow's weeds. That had made her white hair and white skin more unsettling. She couldn't have been more than fifty, but to Travis and me she looked older than the mountains themselves. We had managed to hold onto our rods and reels, but we dropped the stringers of trout at her feet and took off down the creek, splashing and tripping and not daring to look back till we made the river. We'd never fished Wolf Creek again.

When Widow Glendower came to the cabin door she didn't look much different than she'd looked a quarter century before when I'd last seen her.

"You look to be an Alexander," she said.

"Yes," I said, but there was nothing to her knowing that. Anybody in Jocassee would recognize Alexander features.

"You ain't got need for a granny-woman, have you?"

"No," I said. "I'm the high sheriff, and I'm looking for Holland Winchester. I was wondering if you'd seen him?"

"Oh I've seen him," Widow Glendower said. "I seen him twenty-odd years ago when I brung him into this world."

"Have you seen him the last two days?"

"No," she said, saying the word slow as if she was mulling my question over in her head.

"Does he ever come up this way hunting or fishing?"

"No. I'd recall it if I seen him doing such."

I stepped off the porch, knowing I'd wasted my time coming here. Widow Glendower grinned at me.

"Come back and visit any time, Sheriff," she said. "And be sure you let me know if you have need of a granny-woman."

I was short-breathed and my knee needed a rest, but I didn't stop walking until I reached the river. I sat down on a log where I had a good view of the bank and finally saw what I was looking for, the plant Andre Michaux had found in the valley in 1788. The Cherokee called it shee-show. Because it grew close to water, they had believed it could end a drought.

I walked over and kneeled beside the plant whose flowers looked like tiny white bells. I touched the leathery green leaves. De Soto's secretary Rodrigo Rangel had not mentioned the flower in his writings. Neither had Bartram. Michaux had been the first European to see the plant for what it was, something rare and beautiful, submerged from the rest of the world in the valley of the lost.

~

Most of the men had gathered in Billy Holcombe's yard by the time I got back. Stonewall hadn't caught a scent. Tom Watson had brought nothing out of the river but a snapping turtle and a few more trout.

Billy soon called it a day as well. I watched him limp out of his field toward the house where his supper waited. *You don't seem a man luck has found often in his life, Billy,* I thought. *Maybe now that you need it most though, it has finally come. But even the dead can slip free like Houdini from rocks and rope that hold them down. Currents can tug a body out of the deepest undercut. You've read your Bible, Billy,* I thought. *You know the dead can rise on the third day.*

When the last man finally straggled in, I told Leonard and the others who'd walked the woods that I wouldn't be needing them anymore. I told Tom and his men to be back at 9:00 in the morning.

"That body's got to be in the river," I told Bobby as we got in the car.

"Well I don't see how we missed it," Bobby said. "We poked every undercut and dynamited every blue hole a damn mile upstream and down. You think it to be farther away than that?"

"No," I said as we bounced down Billy's drive. "That body can't be too far from that horse," and soon as I said that I realized what Billy Holcombe had done. I laughed out loud at the sheer smarts of it.

"What's tickled your funny bone?" Bobby asked.

"I'll show you."

I turned the car around and headed back up the drive.

"Get a shovel and a rope from the trunk," I told Bobby as we got out.

Bobby did as I told him while I stepped up on the porch.

"Come on," I told Billy when he came to the door. "And bring a lantern. We need to go back over to where your plow horse is."

Billy was worried. I could tell that right away. Lucas Bridges, the county coroner, claimed a dying man or woman had a certain smell about them. I believed a scared man did too, and what I smelled coming off Billy Holcombe was more than sweat from field work.

"Step ahead of us and be the bell-cow," I told Billy as we left the yard. "I'd rather see a snake before I put my foot down on him."

Though rattlesnakes were bad to crawl on hot nights, I was more concerned with Billy trying to slip off in the dark. I wanted him out front where I could watch him.

"What you got on your mind?" Bobby asked.

"Maybe just a snipe hunt, but I don't think so," I said.

We made our way across the river, the same river De Soto had crossed. De Soto hadn't found what he'd been looking for in Jocassee, but, as Michaux had discovered, things could be found in the valley of the lost. All you had to do was look with a careful eye. That and know where to look.

The moon wasn't out, and it took me a moment to realize what that meant. Then a breeze rustled the trees. If the horse hadn't been close by I'd have smelled the sharpness in the air that comes before rain. I wondered if Billy knew the rain was coming. If he did I wondered if he saw it as more good luck. Or did he believe it no longer mattered since I knew now what he'd done with Holland's body? *Yes, Billy, the eyes can lie, but eventually they'll tell the truth. If I could see your eyes they would tell me, Billy. But I'll know soon enough*, I thought as we stepped onto the far bank. Soon enough.

"We got to move that horse," I told Bobby. "Do you think if we put a rope around its neck we could drag it a few yards?"

"We can try," Bobby said.

The buzzards had flown up in the trees to roost for the night, so all Bobby had to scare off was a possum. Bobby tied the rope on, doing his best not to breathe, for the horse was plenty rank after two days under a dog-day sun.

"You help too," I told Billy. We dragged the horse until I said stop. The lantern made the ground shadowy, but there was enough light to see there was no body. I picked up the shovel and stepped closer. Two jabs and I knew that ground hadn't been dug.

"Let's go," I said, "and leave the damn rope, Bobby. I don't feel like smelling dead horse all the way to Seneca."

For a few minutes I had been so certain. But I'd been dead wrong. Now it was as if I was back at the beginning, with nothing certain at all, not even if there had been a murder. Maybe he's not even dead, I thought. Maybe Holland had gotten Amy Holcombe pregnant and taken off to Texas or California. Maybe Bobby was right and Holland was having a good laugh at our expense, that this was Holland's way of getting back at me for what happened at The Borderline—have me come out here and make a fool of myself searching for someone who was alive half a country away.

But I couldn't believe Holland was alive. Billy Holcombe had been expecting me when I stepped into his field. Mrs. Winchester's grief was real. As we recrossed I could smell the coming rain. A real chunk washer, I hoped, enough to raise the dead.

"I'll see you tomorrow," I told Billy as he stepped up on his porch. "Who knows what might turn up, especially after a good rain." Billy said nothing to that. He just went on inside to finish his supper.

"You mind driving?" I asked Bobby.

"Not at all," Bobby said, so I handed him the keys. I closed my eyes as we bumped down toward the river.

"Radio bother you?" Bobby asked.

"No," I said.

Hank Williams' voice rose out of the static, singing about his loneliness. He was a young man, still in his twenties but already rich and famous. I wondered if what he sang was just words to him. His voice argued otherwise. That old, weary voice knew what the high lonesome was. I'd heard Williams was bad to drink. There was something deep inside him that money and fame couldn't cure. I reckoned it must be in a lot of us since his records were so popular. Loneliness was a word you could give it, but it was something beyond words. It was a kind of yearning, a sense that part of your heart was unfilled.

A preacher would say it was man's condition since leaving Eden, and so many of the old hymns were about how in another life we'd be with God. But we lived in the here and now. You tried to find something to fill that absence. Maybe a marriage could cure that yearning, though mine hadn't. Drink did it for many a man besides Williams. Maybe children filled it for some, or maybe like Daddy even the love of a place that connected you to generations of your family.

"Wake up, Sheriff. We're back," Bobby said.

I opened my eyes.

"You go on home, Bobby. I'll meet you here at 8:30."

I went into the office, walking past the cell I thought for a few minutes this evening I was going to fill. The book Mrs. Pipkin had brought lay on my desk. A damp cellar smell rose off the old paper when I opened it. *Travels through North and South Carolina, Georgia, East and West Florida*, the cover page said. Below the title, *By William Bartram.*

The first splats of rain streaked the windows, and though I hadn't even a tomato plant in the ground, memory made my heart lift. I knew Daddy heard that rain, and Travis did too. They would sleep better tonight than they'd slept in weeks.

I knew I should call Janice, but I couldn't make my hands pick up the telephone. Sometime tomorrow I would have to figure out the words I would say to her and then say them, as I had the first time I'd left.

"I'd end up getting drafted anyhow," I'd told her when I joined the Marines in 1941. But I'd wanted to go. I'd wanted to get away from her, away from a life that had been something so different from what had seemed promised, away from my dead-end job in a cotton mill, away from that miscarriage and a marriage that we both knew was a failure. How could it not be when all our union had brought into the world was death.

But I had come back to Seneca and Janice. Maybe it had been a sense of obligation, of knowing that Janice had chosen me when there were plenty of other men from wealthy families she could have had. I now believed it was more than that though. I believed that our lost child had bonded us in ways that outlasted even love.

I opened the brittle pages to Part II, the section where Bartram left Charleston for what would be called for a few more years the Cherokee Nation. I followed his words the way he'd followed the Savannah River upstream to where the land became hills and then mountains. I turned the page, and Bartram was describing the place where my grandfather's great-grandfather had settled twelve years before Bartram passed through that valley.

> *I continued on again three or four miles, keeping on the trading path which led me over uneven rocky land, and crossing rivulets and brooks, rapidly descending over rocky precipices, when I came into a charming vale, embellished with a delightful glittering river, which meandered through it.*

He had been from Scotland, that first Alexander, a man who had fought with Prince Charlie at the battle of Cullodden. He'd come down the Shenandoah Valley. Ian Alexander found his wife in southwest Virginia, a woman named Mary Thomas, who being Welsh would have shared his hatred of the English. He stayed there five years, then came farther south, stopping in this place that surely reminded him of the Scottish midlands where he'd been born. Most of his neighbors were Cherokee, and his oldest son would marry a Cherokee. But soon Colonel Williamson would push the Indians into the high mountains of North Carolina.

My Uncle Thomas had not known which side that first Alexander had supported. He must have seen what the British were doing to the Cherokee was the same thing they'd done to the Scots, but with the Indians gone there would be more land for whites like him. More interesting, what had his son done? Did he fight with his wife's people or against them? Something had happened, but it was lost now in the valley's past.

Bartram did not mention meeting anyone as he'd passed through Jocassee that spring day. But I wondered if Ian Alexander had stood in a field and watched Bartram as he rode his horse along the trading path. Perhaps Old Ian acknowledged the white stranger with a wave, perhaps a meal offered and accepted.

I read on, following Bartram as he moved northwest and crossed what would someday be a state line. He'd stopped and rested at the top of Oconee Mountain. Turning to look back on the land he'd traversed that day, Bartram had described what he saw. *The mountainous wilderness appearing undulated as the great ocean after a tempest*, he'd written, as if he'd witnessed the valley buried under a huge, watery silence two centuries before it would happen.

Like Michaux, Bartram was a naturalist. He understood that things disappeared. Maybe that was why he'd felt compelled to preserve with sketches and words everything he saw, from Cherokee council-houses to buffalo bones. He wanted to get it all down. He wanted things to be remembered.

I lay the book down. The rain drummed against the roof and the town was quiet and still. I was tired, tireder than I'd been in a long time. I went into the cell and lay down on the cot.

I dreamed of water deep as time.

Sunlight streaked through the bars when I woke. The telephone was ringing, so I stumbled out of the cell to my desk.

"Daddy's had another heart attack," Travis said.

"Where is he?"

"Over here at the hospital."

"I'll be there in five minutes," I said.

I wrote a note telling Bobby to go on up to Jocassee and start dragging the river, that I'd join them soon as I could.

At the hospital I found Travis and Laura slouched in plastic chairs. The twins lay on the couches.

"How bad is it?" I asked Travis.

"The doctor says he might live a day or two, but he ain't going to leave here alive."

"What happened?"

"Shank of the evening I went over to work some more on his roof. I figured he was mending fence so I didn't start no searching till near dark. I found him in the far pasture."

Travis looked at the floor.

"I thought he was dead. It'd be better if he had been."

"Did you try to call me last night?"

"No," Travis said, still looking at the floor.

"Why the hell not?"

Travis looked up, his gray eyes meeting mine.

"You ain't given a damn about him for so long I didn't think you'd want your sleep bothered."

I grabbed the front of his shirt, lifting him out of the chair. My knuckles pressed against his breast bone.

"You don't know a thing of what I feel."

"You're right," Travis said, his eyes still looking straight into mine. "I knew once but not anymore."

The room seemed to close in around us. Whatever my life had been and was to be had come to this moment when I held my fist against Travis's chest.

"No, Will," Travis said, his eyes no longer looking into mine but looking behind me.

I turned and saw my nephew, my namesake, with a pocketknife sprouting from his fist, the other twin beside him, hands clenched.

"Put it down, son," Travis said.

"Not till he lets you go," Will said.

I opened my fist, stepped back. The room's white walls widened again. We all stood there for a minute, sharing nothing but the same name.

"Will they let me see him?"

"Yeah," Travis said, rubbing his chest. "They'll let you."

"You might need this," Laura said, and handed me a hospital pass.

I showed the pass to the nurse on the second floor, and she led me to the room. Daddy lay stretched out on the bed, his eyes staring at the ceiling, tubes taped to both arms. His skin was tinged blue, each breath an effort. Travis was right. It would have been better if he'd died in his fields, feeling the land against his body, seeing trees and crops and a sky that promised rain.

"We're trying to make him comfortable," the nurse said.

"Does he know I'm here?"

"I don't know. Maybe."

The nurse left the room.

I held Daddy's hand, and I knew it for a dead man's hand. It was that cold. A hand that did not acknowledge mine. His eyes stayed fixed on the ceiling. His body was nothing more than a husk now. I prayed for his soul, but he didn't need my prayers. He'd lived a good life and treated people a lot better than they'd sometimes treated him.

"I'm sorry, Daddy," I said aloud.

And I was, but it was too late to matter. He was gone from me now and never coming back. I held his hand until the nurse came back in to change his sheets.

"I'll be back this evening," I told Travis. "Leave a message with Janice if something happens."

Travis nodded. He knew my meaning.

I drove on up into the mountains, a blue sky overhead, but

plenty of rain had fallen. The creeks ran quick and muddy. The fields were no longer dust. It had been a soaking rain, the answer to prayers and dead black snakes and shee-show and whatever else people had found to believe in.

Billy wasn't in his fields, but I hadn't expected him to be since it was too muddy to get much done anyway. *You might get some corn and beans after all, Billy*, I thought as I followed the other men's muddy footprints down the field edge to the river. Already the corn stalks seemed to be standing taller, the beans greener.

The river was high, fast and muddy like the creeks. Crossing was a lot trickier than yesterday. I found a limb to use as a staff and took my time. I gave a shout, and Bobby answered downstream. The water was too high to use the grappling hooks. All Bobby and the rest of the men were doing was hoping to find what water had already brought up on its own.

By eleven the river crested. Tom and Leonard cast the grappling hooks into blue holes as the rest of us walked the banks. The river had washed up tree limbs and a tractor tire and even a rod and reel. But it still hid Holland. We stopped at noon and ate donuts and drank Cheerwines Bobby had brought.

"If that storm didn't bring that body up I don't know what the hell will," Bobby said as we sat on the bank.

"It sure enough brought up most everything else," Tom said.

We watched the river flow past, almost as clear now as it had been the day before and not much higher.

It was the river I'd been baptized in.

"Washed in the blood of the lamb," Preacher Robertson had said as the blue sky fell away and water rushed over me. It seemed Preacher Robertson held me there forever, but I hadn't been afraid. I was ten years old. I had felt the power of that river and believed it nothing less than God Himself swirling around me.

After we ate, Tom and Leonard worked the blue holes while

Bobby and me waded in and poked bamboo poles under banks and between big rocks. All we found was snakes and muskrats.

"Let's go," I said at four o'clock. We recrossed the river and slogged our way back up the field edge.

"You go on back with Tom and the others," I told Bobby when we got to the cars. "I'll be along directly."

I watched Tom's car disappear around a bend, then stepped into Billy Holcombe's yard. I heard a rasping sound coming from the woodshed and walked over and peered inside. At first I saw nothing, but my eyes began to adjust to the dark. Billy slowly took his form behind what looked like prison bars. Like a haint shape-shifting, my older kin would have said. But I was the ghost, haunting a valley where I no longer belonged.

Soon I saw the bars he worked on were wood, not steel. He hummed to himself, so soft it sounded no louder than a wasp's drone. I could smell the wood, wild cherry, and I knew the crib was as much for his wife as for the child. Whatever had happened between Holland and her, the crib was a sign she and Billy had gotten past it. She had stuck by him the last few days, lied for him. Whatever had happened that morning, she'd had to make a choice between Holland and Billy and she'd chosen Billy.

Billy kept on humming, and I bet he didn't even know he was doing it. I listened to a man who believed his future was going to be better than his past, a man who'd woke up to rain-soaked fields and the knowledge come fall he'd have a bumper crop. A man about to learn he'd gotten away with murder.

I wondered what would happen when Carolina Power ran him off his land. Billy's parents had been sharecroppers. This land didn't connect Billy to his family the way Daddy's land connected him to ours. Billy's land signaled a break from his past, from what his family had been. Maybe land to Billy was just something to be used, like a truck or plow horse.

Billy might think his ship had come in when Carolina Power bought his place for a few dollars an acre more than he'd paid for it, at least until he saw the price of a farm like his in another part of the county. Maybe he'd take that money to Seneca or Anderson and buy a house with an indoor toilet and electricity and think he'd found paradise. He'd work in a mill where he'd get a paycheck at the end of every week and not have to worry anymore about drought and hail and tobacco worms.

Other changes he wouldn't like as much, things that would make him miss being behind a horse and plow. He'd have to ask permission to get a drink of water or take a piss. The work would be the same thing day after day, week after week, the mill hot and humid as dog days all year round. He'd breathe an unending drizzle of lint he'd spend half his nights coughing back up.

His work would give him no satisfaction, but he'd have a wife and child to go home to when the mill whistle freed him at day's end. There were men who would envy that about him if nothing else.

As for my life, it was in Seneca. My morning telephone call had woke me up in more than one way. It had been a reminder of something I had already known despite what I'd been able to pretend for a few hours—I had chosen my life long ago when I had picked up a fork, picked it up in a house I had believed to be solid and permanent as anything on earth.

But nothing is solid and permanent. Our lives are raised on the shakiest foundations. You don't need to read history books to know that. You only have to know the history of your own life.

I watched Billy through the bars, knowing in a few minutes I'd drive out of this valley. I'd look in my rearview mirror and watch the land disappear as if sinking into water.

When I had become a deputy I had made out my will and stipulated that I was to be buried here in Jocassee with the other Alexanders. I hoped I would be in that grave before they built the reservoir so when the water rose it would rise over me and Daddy and Momma and over Old Ian Alexander and his wife Mary and over the lost body of the princess named Jocassee and the Cherokee mounds and the trails De Soto and Bartram and Michaux had followed and the meadows and streams and forests they had described and all would forever vanish and our faces and names and deeds and misdeeds would be forgotten as if we and Jocassee had never been.

I wish you well, Billy, I thought. I stepped closer and blotted out most of his light.

"You got away with it," I said and left him there, his hands shaping the future.

the WIFE

AT FIRST it was just a kind of joke between me and the older women. They'd lay a hand on my belly and say something silly like "Is there a biscuit in the oven" or "I don't feel nothing blossoming yet." Then we'd all have a laugh. Or a woman more my own age might say, "A latch-pin can poke holes in the end of them things," or "Nuzzle up to him of a sudden in the barn or the field edge and that will do the trick." Such words made me blush for they brought up notions I'd never known women to talk of out amongst each other.

Me and Billy hadn't wanted a baby right away. We had a full enough portion just getting used to one another so he wore a sheath each time he put himself inside me. As that first year passed we settled in and got easy and comfortable in our marriage, the way a good team of horses learns to work together and help each other out.

We had a good harvest that fall and got ourselves a little ahead and our second winter together a night came when I said "You don't have to wear it" and he knew my meaning. That night as we shared our bodies the love was so much better, for the hope of a baby laid down with us.

The weeks went by and I didn't get the morning sickness or tired easy or any of the other signs. Then it was six months and then our third anniversary. We held each other most every night but when the curse was on me. Yet it didn't seem to do no good. The older women still made their comments but they wasn't as funny now and I suspicioned they wasn't meant to be.

"It's time you started your family," they'd say, like as if it was their business to tell me such.

The younger girls, girls I'd grown up with, would make a show of their young ones whenever I was around.

"Ain't she a darling," they'd say to me or, "You want to hold him?"

They all every one of them seemed to be saying to me I wasn't a woman till I had a young one of my own.

"Are you and Billy getting along?" Momma finally asked one afternoon when she came to visit.

"Yes, Momma," I said. "We're getting on fine."

But Momma was doubtful of my words. She looked out the window where Billy was drawing water for Sam.

"A marriage ain't no simple thing to keep sprightly. It takes some tending to."

"I know that, Momma," I said.

"I bought you some things," Momma said, and took some lipstick and cheek rouge from her pocket. "A man likes his wife to pretty up for him sometimes."

"I don't need you to buy me such things, Momma," I said, but she pressed them in my hand.

"You make yourself up with that lipstick and cheek rouge," Momma said. "And put on that blue dress to show off your eyes. You do that tonight, Amy. It'll make a difference. I'm certain of that."

But Momma was wrong. It made no difference at all.

When it came December me and Billy finally went to Seneca to see Doctor Wilkins. We sat there most forever before the nurse called our names.

"You can go out to the waiting room if you like," Doctor Wilkins told Billy after a few minutes.

"No," Billy said. "I'll stay."

Doctor Wilkins put me in his stirrups. He laid a sheet over my legs and opened me up.

"No tumors or infection," Doctor Wilkins said. "That's a good sign."

Then he took what looked to be ice tongs and opened me way wider. He put a tube in and blew into that tube while he listened. I gasped for the pain of it.

I looked over at Billy and his face was studying the far wall.

"Everything looks to be fine," Doctor Wilkins said.

Doctor Wilkins opened his desk and reached Billy a sheath.

"I guess you know what I need," Doctor Wilkins said. "There are some magazines in the back bathroom. When you finish bring it back and I'll put it under the microscope."

Billy got all red and shame-faced but he did what was asked of him. Then Doctor Wilkins looked under the microscope. He stared long and careful and that was sure no good sign.

He finally took his eyeball off the microscope.

"I can't find a single live sperm," he said.

Going back home that afternoon was ever a long and silent ride. I looked out the window and the world seemed dead. The mountains was bald-looking and brown, the trees shucked of their leaves, nothing more than skeletons of what they'd been in summer. I looked out on those bare mountains and a memory I'd been trying for months to keep pushed deep in my mind corked up to the surface and wouldn't go back down.

It was a memory of me and my brother Matthew and the day

I broke his body. We'd been in the barn loft doing the work Daddy had sent us there to do. At least I was doing it. Matthew was being contrary and not doing nothing but sassing. I was twelve and him only eight. It vexed me to have to do it all.

"Get on over there and do your part, Matthew," I'd said, and shoved him toward the other bales. He'd tried to keep his balance and tottered back to where the loft window laid open like a trap door. He took that last step backwards and it was like he'd just stepped off the edge of a cliff hang.

Momma and Daddy hadn't punished me for what had happened, never spoke a word of blame about it. Yet I'd blamed myself plenty. Those first couple of days when Doctor Griffen wasn't sure what might happen in the long run I'd wished more than anything in my life it had been me that fell through the window loft. When Doctor Griffen said Matthew would walk again that made it bearable but just barely.

What bothered my thoughts was that as much punishment as I'd heaped on myself for what happened, maybe God figured it wasn't enough. I'd near killed a young one once and I'd not be trusted with another.

For a while I tried to make myself believe that things would be all right, that Billy was a good man and two people could have a good life without young ones. Yet it hurt each Sunday when me and Billy went to church and all the others of our age had their babies or when we went to Momma and Daddy's and Ginny's two young ones filled up the house with a happiness only children can bring. Afterwards when me and Billy went home, our house seemed quiet and empty. Billy felt it too. I knew he blamed himself. If I felt less a woman for having no baby, I knew he felt less a man for not being able to plant his seed in me.

Billy spoke not a word about what we'd found out from Doctor Wilkins but the knowledge laid over our house like a pall. We couldn't talk about it. What was the good when words couldn't change what laid on our hearts. I'd had to talk of it to someone though so one Sunday after noon-dinner when Billy and Daddy was out at the barn I told Momma and Ginny what Doctor Wilkins had said.

"And he claimed there was nothing to be done?" Momma asked.

"Yes ma'am," I said, and saying it out loud made it all the more certain.

"Oh, Amy," Momma said.

She took me in her arms and cried for me.

"Doctors don't know everything," Ginny said, her voice cold as a creek stone. "There's them who has a learning you don't get out of books, a knowledge no man has the least notion of."

"What are you talking around, Ginny?" I asked.

"I'm saying there's one person with the knowing of how to cure what no town doctor can."

"Maybe it's best to just let things be, Amy," Momma said, for she knew the what and who Ginny's talk was sidling toward.

"That old woman knows things," Ginny said. "She might could help Amy."

"Don't you go and see that old woman," Momma said. "If you and Billy ain't meant to have young ones it's the Lord's will. Why you and Billy got other things for to..."

Momma didn't finish for she caught sight of Billy standing on the other side of the screen door.

"It could have been you with the problem," Billy said as he drove us back home. "If it was I'd have never gone blabbing about it all over the valley. Maybe it is something wrong with you. For all I know that doctor didn't have no reckoning of what was wrong. He was liable to say near anything to get his five dollars."

Billy's neck vein pronged out like a dousing stick. He gripped the steering wheel like it was something he wanted to choke to death.

"Spread it around just to make sure that everybody knows it's my failing and not yours."

"That ain't what I was doing, Billy," I said.

"Damn you to hell for talking of it with others," Billy said.

He'd never near spoke such a thing to me before. He'd not said it to the hail when it beat down his tobacco or to the cow when it hoofed him and cracked his rib. But he'd said it to me.

The next Sunday at church it was clear Momma had scattered words to the other women about me and Billy. Billy saw it too and there was fury in his eyes for the women and for me. Each sad-mouthed word or ruthful look unyoked us a little more.

"You poor dear," Martha Whitmire said and hugged me to her.

"It's a stout burden for any woman to carry," Sue Burrell added, looking all sorrowful.

I knew Momma meant well but her telling the others made it harder. What those women meant to be pity seemed to me little more than gloating. That was a hard-hearted way to think about other folks and in the deepest part of me I knew it wasn't just the other women I'd turned hard-hearted toward. I stood up with the others and mouthed the old hymns like I always did but those words stirred me no more now than they would a barn rat. He'd given a passel of young ones to every other woman in that church but allowed me never a one, though I'd prayed hard morning and night now for a year. How could He give my momma nine and my sister not yet eighteen two and leave me fallow as a December corn field. If I was being punished for what happened to Matthew, that was wrong. How could something I did at twelve, something that was more accident than meanness, be grudged against me for the rest of my life? Not a sparrow falls from the sky without His knowledge, the Bible claimed. Don't that include children that fall from a loft, I told myself.

~

"Don't you go and see that old woman," Momma said, but I did go, on a January morning when snow laid on the path that followed the river upstream, the river getting faster and skinny, beech trees and rocks looming on each side of the trail as the gorge got narrower like a giant book that's slow getting shut. Or maybe more like a steel leg-hold trap, I thought, looking up at the big rocks that jagged out over me like teeth. The land got dark and shadowy because the sun couldn't get in without it was full noon, clumps of mistletoe the only color in the trees. I'd once heard my granddaddy claim the Cherokees had stayed clear of this place, wouldn't even hunt here.

It was easy enough to figure why the few folks who'd lived here called this part of the gorge The Dismal, because you couldn't help but feel that way as you passed through. I walked by the old Chapman place that was now nothing but a stone chimney. It looked like a tombstone there all by itself with no cabin to surround it.

Where Wolf Creek poured into the river I saw Luke Murphree's place. His house still stood but the boards was gray and wormy, the tin roof brown like November leaves. Grandma had told me how Luke's property had bumped up against Widow Glendower's land and he'd not bothered to fence his cattle in. They'd been bad to wander onto the old woman's place and eat her apples and trample her beans.

Then one May the cattle started getting sick. Daddy allowed it was from eating the leaves of a cherry tree Luke had felled. Others said blackleg. But Luke swore his cattle had been hexed. Whatever it was six cows died that May, and soon enough after Luke and his family followed the Chapmans out of the hollow. No one else moved in.

Nor likely to, Grandma had said.

Glendower was up here by herself now, for she had no kin as far as anyone on the river knew. There had been many another story about her I'd heard growing up. How once Lindsey Kilgore saw her rise out of a trout pool he'd been fishing, her body forming itself out of the water. And Janey Suttles saw her in a graveyard, the grave flowers turning brown and wilting like as if frost-bit wherever her shadow fell.

I'd heard all such tales from Grandma, on a winter night when me and the other young ones huddled up near the fireplace. Wind had been whipping through the gorge and the limbs of the big beech scratching the tin roof like something trying to get in. Grandma had told us the ways of witches and the signs of them, everything of what they could do to you and you to them.

We kids was so scared we wouldn't head up the stairs to bed without Daddy going first. Daddy scoffed and told us Granny was just pulling our leg, that there wasn't no such thing as witches, that Widow Glendower was a harmless old soul who'd learned to doctor with roots and leaves and tree bark back when folks had to tend to their own selves when they got sick.

"That old woman has helped many another person when they wasn't no one else to doctor them and now some of them same people call her a witch," Daddy said as he tucked the quilts around us.

But after he'd snuffed the lamp and went downstairs I couldn't help wondering why if he argued there was no such thing as witches he'd nailed a horseshoe upside down above the front door the first day he and Momma had moved into this house. And why he'd never had a notion to take it down.

The trail followed the creek deeper into the hollow. Beech trees got thicker, snuffing out more of what little light dribbled in. Soon rocks big as haystacks skinnied the trail. I kept my eyes up. Some of the old folks claimed there was still a few panthers around and this seemed as likely a spot to find one as any. All of everything was quiet, even the creek as it flowed under a skimming of ice. A part of me wanted to point my feet in the other direction, follow Wolf Creek back down to the river and on home. I kept hoofing up the path. I wanted a baby and Widow Glendower was near the last hope I had of getting one.

I had no reckoning of how far up the creek she lived but after I passed the big rocks the woods opened up. I saw smoke and then the chimney and then the cabin itself. A black dog big as a calf wiggled out from under the porch and barked as I stepped across the walk-log. Then it disappeared back under the cabin. Widow Glendower opened the door and came out on the porch.

"Who be you?" she asked. Her voice was raspy, like her throat had clotted over with rust from not being used.

"Amy," I said, and almost spoke Boone instead of Holcombe.

"Amy Holcombe," Widow Glendower said, saying it slow and thoughtful-like.

"I was a Boone before I married. My Daddy's Randall Boone."

"From over near Tamassee?"

"Yes ma'am."

"And Lillie Boone is your grandma."

"Yes ma'am," I said. "Me and my husband Billy live down the river now. Our land borders Sarah Winchester's place."

"I know Sarah," Widow Glendower said. "I cured her of the thrush a while back. I caught her young ones too. That youngest boy, he come late. He was so husky he near killed his momma before I got him into the world. He back from soldiering yet?"

"He's been back for a couple of months now," I said.

"Step closer, girl," Widow Glendower said.

I walked up to the first step. She wore a gingham dress wrinkly as her face, a black shawl on her bony shoulders. Her back-bone bowed and made her lean a ways over herself. She reminded me of something with that stooped body and the black shawl hanging down from her shoulders. Hanging like wings, I thought. Then I knew what it was she favored.

We passed no words for a minute as she studied over me. I studied over her as well, her eyes gray and hard-seeming as granite tombstones, her skin paled white as a mushroom stem, white as the fish I once saw in a cave, fish that had swam in the dark so long they'd lost all their color and even their eyes. Her hair was white as her face, long and tangly like it hadn't been combed in years. To make people fancy you a witch you could do no better, I thought.

My thoughts must have showed plain as the mistletoe I'd seen in the trees.

"You ain't feared of me, are you?" she asked.

I didn't rightly know how to answer, for either way seemed wrong.

She smiled then, and I saw for all her years she still had teeth. They wasn't black and gnarly but white and not a one missing. It seemed a warm smile and I remembered what Daddy had said about her helping the sick when there'd been no one else.

"You been listening to slack talk if you are, girl, listening to folks what will say the worst of anyone who keeps to theirselves. What they claiming me for, a witch?"

"I never believed such," I said.

"No," Widow Glendower said. "You wouldn't. You seem a girl with more smarts than to believe a silly something like that."

She tightened the shawl around her neck.

"It's too cold to stand here and visit. You come inside."

She turned and stepped through the door, not looking back to see if I followed.

I walked into a front room dour like a root cellar, the only light yellow hearth-flames that licked the bottom of a copper kettle.

"Set your body down," she said and nodded at a split-cane chair by the hearth. She leaned into the fire and lifted the kettle, then stepped into the other room.

My eyes started to find their way in the dark. I looked around the room. There wasn't much of anything besides another split-cane chair on the other side of the hearth. No clock ticked on the fire-board and there wasn't a lamp or a single picture or a Bible. A trunk made of ash wood laid in the far corner, its top painted blue like as if someone had started a job they hadn't troubled to finish.

Widow Glendower came back in the room with two tin cups in her hand.

"Here," she said as she reached me a cup. "Most folks can't hazard how often a time something warm can cure what ails a body."

I laid the cup on my lap, my hands holding it steady. The coffee looked the color of the river after spring rains.

"Taste of it," Widow Glendower said, raising her cup to her lips.

I raised mine as well and felt the steam of it on my face. I took a sip and felt it slide down my throat and warm all over where the cold had crept into me. I couldn't help but shut my eyes a minute and savor that comforting.

"So what fetches you to my door?" Widow Glendower asked.

I didn't dawdle with my words. I'd already walked too far and lived with it too long not to take the short path.

"Doctor Wilkins, he says me and Billy can't have a young one. I gave myself a thought you might could help us."

Widow Glendower leveled her gray eyes on mine. They was old eyes but clear and steady. I reckoned they could still see most everything they wanted to.

"I know a few things no town-doctor knows," she said. "Is it you or your man got the problem?"

"It's Billy."

Widow Glendower looked into the fire.

"There's things that might could help," she said. "But let's drink our coffee first."

So we sipped our coffee and stared at the fire, neither me or her offering up a word till we finished. That's the devil's tongue reaching up out of hell, my Grandma had said of hearth-flames when I was growing up. I wasn't wanting to mull on such a thing now.

Widow Glendower laid our empty cups on the fire-board. She walked into the back room and got a poke, then went over to the trunk. She talked at herself while she grabbled around inside, stopping to put some one thing or another in the poke.

"There's bloodroot and mandrake root, some sang too," she said, handing me the poke. "Brew up a tea with them for your man."

"What if that ain't the thing for to make it take?"

"Come planting time wait for a waxing moon. Take every stitch of clothes off and lay down with him in a field that's fresh seeded. I reckon you exact what I mean by laying down with him."

"Yes ma'am," I said, and I felt my face blush up red as a moonseed berry.

I knew it to be getting darksome soon. I needed to be headed back home but I wanted something more certain sure than roots and laying down in fields.

"I've heard it told you know what hasn't yet been," I said.

Widow Glendower stared at the flames like she was reading them.

"I've saw things that come to pass, things that someday will. I've saw a time when the dead will raise from their graves, a time the river will drown this whole valley."

She looked at me and smiled.

"But you ain't wanting to ponder such things as that right now. You want to know if you'll birth a young one."

"Yes ma'am."

"I believe you will."

Widow Glendower got up from her chair.

"You best be getting toward home, girl. There's little enough light left to get you there."

I reached my hand around my dress pocket till I fished out a silver dollar.

"I brung this for to pay with," I said.

Widow Glendower shook her head.

"I don't want your money," she said. "You buy that baby of yours a play-pretty with that dollar."

"Well, I thank you," I said and left her there on the porch.

I stepped pretty lively the way back down to the river for that old woman had gave me a pail-full of hope when I'd had but a dry well before. It was the shank of evening. The sky was gray and sleety looking but the world somehow seemed brighter. I took more notice at the liveness you could find if you kept your eyes searching for it, not just the mistletoe in the big oaks but a hemlock or white pine deep off in the woods, the Christmas ferns and hairy-cat moss on Wolf Creek's banks and the ground pine poking out from dead leaves.

I was halfway home when it happened. A shadow came over me and then a shiver so deep down in my bones it could be but one thing. I looked up. No cloud passed overhead, not even a hawk or crow, and I knew somebody had crossed over my grave. Don't go to dwelling on death, think about new life, I told myself. I tightened the shawl around my neck and walked on.

It was coming dark when I passed near the Winchesters' house. Through the window I could see Holland and his momma eating their supper. I'd passed words with Mrs. Winchester a few times but never a word with Holland.

"It's best to stay clear of Holland Winchester," Billy had said soon as Holland got back from the war. "He's never been nothing but trouble."

So I had, making sure I did my house chores when he worked next to our land. But as I did my sweeping and such I'd peek a look at him through the curtains. He was a big-muscled man, a man many another wouldn't want to cross words with, but he wasn't as rough-looking as I'd of thought to hear how others spoke of him. There was some handsome in his features and I wondered why some girl hadn't made him a husband. But then I reckoned Holland wasn't a settling-down kind of man.

"Where you been off to?" Billy fretted when I stepped through the door. "A plate of food ought not be asking too much after I've been in the fields all day."

I told him where I'd been and the why.

"Had to make sure that old woman hadn't missed the gossip about me not able to seed you," Billy said all spiteful-like. "Afraid there might be a soul in Jocassee didn't know."

"She maybe can help us, Billy," I said. "She gave me roots to make a tea."

"I ain't seeing how some yarbing could make a difference, especially from what Doctor Wilkins told us," Billy said.

"It wouldn't likely hurt us to try," I said. "You could at least hear me out."

There was some moody in my voice too. It was like our words was clouds gathering up for a storm.

"It'll do no good. I'm certain sure of that," Billy said.

Yet he listened and that argued much as anything that he was as wanting of a baby as I was. I showed him the roots and he drank the tea I made from them each morning and night with no fuss. When spring came we laid down naked under the waxing moon.

Those nights Billy tried to plant his seed in me I watched the moon round up and swell like I hoped my belly would. I wished on that moon like it had been a shooting star or the luckiest rabbit's foot. There in that field with the dirt and dew cold on our skin me and Billy clinged and shivered against one another like we was caught in a flood and holding on each other to keep from getting swept away. It seemed things had gotten about that despairing for us. If they hadn't we wouldn't have been in that field doing what we was doing.

Come the turn of the calendar when it was near my time of the month, me and Billy got more silent than usual around each other, not just our words but things like dropping a piece of firewood in the hearth or slamming the door. We walked soft like we had us a sleeping baby already. Me and Billy somehow notioned if we was quiet and careful enough it would help that new life take root. But the curse came each month anyway and that's what it was, a curse. A curse on me and Billy, a curse on our marriage.

Each time my blood flowed it seemed it was our hearts' blood that was flowing, like our hearts that had once swelled so full of love for one another was shriveling like tomatoes in a drought. We went on about our lives, Billy out in the fields, me doing what needed to be done around the house and barn. There'd been a time when we'd get lonesome for one another and make up a reason for him to come back to the house or me to join him in the field.

"Would it be much bother to help me fetch some water?" I'd ask.

Or maybe Billy would call me out to the field.

"Look here," he'd say, and show me a garnet or arrowhead.

But we kept our distance most all the day now. For the first time since me and Billy had lived here that farm was a lonesome place. When we sat down for supper the food always seemed cold and leftover though I'd just spooned it off the stove. We'd be wore down from the day's work but it wasn't that good tired you get when you reckon your work realizes some good for another besides yourself.

It was April when I walked back up Wolf Creek. All around me the land smelled bright and newborn. Dogwood blossoms brighted up the woods and beard tongue and trout lilies made the path like the prettiest necklace. Red birds and robins sang from branches next to their nests. New life looked to be everywhere but in my belly.

The dog didn't bark this time, just sat on its haunches like it remembered me, then sauntered into the woods. Smoke curled out of the chimney but when I knocked on the door there wasn't no answer. I sat down on the porch and waited, smelling the primroses that bloomed next to the steps.

Widow Glendower finally came back, toting a poke bulged out with what I figured to be roots. When I stood up her eyes fell full on my belly. She stepped closer and rubbed the flat of her hand where her eyes had been looking.

"So it didn't take," she said in a matter-of-fact tone of voice that made me wonder if she ever thought it would. She shuffled past me with the poke still in her hand.

"Come in the house," she said, so I followed her. She laid the poke beside the ash wood chest and told me to have a sit in the same split-cane chair I had last time. Widow Glendower took the copper kettle from the hearth and went into the back room. She came back directly with the same tin cups as last time.

She put the coffee in my hands and sat down in the other chair.

"Taste of it," she said, and I wanted to pinch myself. Everything done or said was the exact as in January and I felt I was snagged up in a dream or a memory and somehow or another it was like it was Widow Glendower's dream more than mine. I didn't find that feeling a bit settling and I gave a heavy sort of thought to putting that coffee down and getting clear of that cabin once and forever.

But I didn't. I took a sip of the coffee, felt its warming all the way to my belly, a belly where no new life waxed. I started tearing up then. All of everything that had happened and not happened in the last couple of years raised up in me like spring rains. It was a hopeless kind of tears, like what you'd shed at a wake or graveyard.

"There ain't nothing to be done about it, is there?" I asked.

She didn't answer at first. She sipped her coffee and looked into the fire like she was mulling something over.

"There's a thing to be done," Widow Glendower finally said. "A simple thing if you have want enough to do it."

"I'll do any or everything to get a baby."

"Will you now," she said, like she doubted me.

"Yes," I said.

"Then it's a easy thing, easy enough you should have figured it out your own self."

Widow Glendower wasn't looking at the fire no more. She was looking flush at me.

"You got a man who can't give you a baby, so you got to lay down with a man who can, and the man who can give you that baby ain't no farther from you than the next farm."

You're a terrible old woman to say such a thing, I thought, but I didn't say it out loud.

"I couldn't never do something like that," I said.

"Then you don't want a baby near bad as you put on."

Widow Glendower's words was cold and hard as winter turnips, and the least kindness had left her face.

"Billy couldn't never forgive me doing such a thing," I said.

"Can you forgive him if you don't have a baby? Can you reckon he will forgive himself?"

It was like she'd laid bare my heart's secretest place, for I knew the truth of her words soon as I heard them, a truth I'd tried to hide from my own self.

I looked into the fire, looked at it the way Widow Glendower did, like as if I could find answers inside. I watched the flickering yellow flames a long time, thinking how when you looked at fire it was like looking at moving water, both ever changing and not changing all at the same time. Sweat started beading my brow like I was fevered. I felt like I did have a fever for my mind was fretful with a lot of things both real and not real. Not real at least for right now.

"You'd give me a charm to bring him to me?" I asked.

Widow Glendower laughed.

"A girl as fetching as you has got considerable enough charms of her own. All you got to do is let him see them charms, see all of them. He'll give you a baby."

"You promise?" I said.

"Oh, for certain I can promise that."

I got up from my chair.

"I don't know that I can do such a thing."

"I think you can," Widow Glendower said, standing up and reaching the cup from my hand. "And you will."

I reached into my dress pocket.

"I brung you this," I said and held out a jar of blackberry jam. "I owe you and figured if you wouldn't take no money you'd take a little something like jam."

"I'm not partial to blackberries," Widow Glendower said. "If you want to make us square even with each other, let me midwife that baby when the time comes."

"All right," I said, hardly giving a thought to what I was saying, for the most part of me still had no real believing it would happen.

"It'll be a joyous time and I'd not want to miss it," Widow Glendower said as she walked me to the door. "I'll be a good granny-woman for you and that baby."

I followed Wolf Creek back down to the river, the water swift and over its banks like even the smallest rivulet most always is in April. The river was high too, high enough the walk-log below Wadakoe Pool was near level with the water. Billy would be coming in from the fields soon for the sun was near noon high, but there'd be no plate of cornbread and beans waiting for him.

I hadn't told him I was off to see Widow Glendower. In the last few weeks if I offered her name or her notions he spoke harsh against her, saying I never should of gone to her in the first place. He held it much against her that what she'd told us hadn't worked. But it was more than that. She showed us both how hoping we was for a child, doing things many another person would of scoffed at as silly superstition, maybe even ungodly.

"That old woman had a good laugh on us," Billy had said. "She played us for fools."

The land evened out. Even blind I'd of known I was nearly home. I left the river so if Billy was in the fields he'd not see me. I cut through woods that was on Mrs. Winchester's property instead.

I was almost onto our land when I heard what sounded like gun shots on the high ground a ways up the ridge. I stepped out of the trees so I could have a better look-see. A man with no shirt on hammered barbed wire to fresh-sawed fence posts. I knew it could be but one man.

At that moment I couldn't help but notion Widow Glendower had somehow put him there, and though I'd walked two miles and worked up a good lather of sweat I felt somebody had run a big icicle down my spine.

I watched him strike another staple, far enough away that the sound followed a couple of seconds later. He stepped a few feet to the next fence post and I saw he was going to run that fence down the line between his Momma's property and ours. I knew in a couple of days he'd work his way down that ridge and be working right beside the house.

You ain't decided nothing yet, I told myself as I walked on into the yard. I can do or not do anything.

But I knew the moment I stepped back in the house that was a lie. There was a coldness no fire or spring weather could shuck off. Billy sat at the table, eating cold cornbread I'd fixed the night before.

By his plate was a glass of milk he'd got from the springhouse. He didn't look up when I came in.

"I'm sorry I didn't have you nothing ready," I said. "I went looking for some flowers to pretty up the place but I couldn't find none."

I reckoned that was the first lie I ever told Billy. It wasn't a much convincing lie but he hardly paid any mind to it. He finished his cornbread and swallowed the last of his milk.

"I'll fix us something special tonight, maybe a pie or cobbler," I said.

"I got to get back in the field," he said, and walked out the door without another word more.

I sat at the table and nibbled at a piece of the cornbread but I hadn't the least appetite so laid it back in the bread box. I listened to Holland's hammer up on the ridge. It no longer sounded like gunshots but a telegraph sending a message, a message I might soon enough answer.

For the next two days I washed clothes and cooked and fed the chickens and all the other chores but my mind was careless. A part of me always listened to Holland tapping his way closer and closer. I idled by my looking glass more too.

Come the second morning I planted a dogwood in the yard, picking a place where Holland would likely see me. It wasn't the time of year to do such a thing but I reckoned it might have a chance of living. I got the shovel from the shed. I dug my hole and walked into the woods and picked out a stout-looking sapling. I rooted it in the hole, then packed the dirt good and watered it.

While I worked I'd glance up the ridge ever so often and see Holland, close enough now to see his big shoulders, the black hair thick on his head. He came steady closer and soon I saw the muscles in his arms and hair on his chest. I knew he saw me by now too. I made myself a natural sight around the yard and there was moments I felt his eyes full upon me.

He never came to church with his momma and I wondered if he even knew my first name. Mrs. Winchester had probably told him, told him that while he'd been off fighting in Korea Billy Holcombe had married a girl named Amy. He probably hadn't cared one way or another. Now I was trying to change that not caring each time I stepped into the yard.

Something is going to happen come morning, I told myself that second night while I laid in bed not able to sleep, and when it does life ain't never again going to be what it has been. There was a scariness in knowing that change was coming but there was a craving as well, like change was something I'd been starved for ever such a long time. Now it had been laid out before me where all I need do was reach out my arms and it was mine. Billy laid beside me but faraway in his dreams. He muttered something but I couldn't make it out. I nuzzled closer to him, my lips next to his ear.

"Whatever I do is for the both of us, Billy," I whispered. "If there was another way, if there just was. But there ain't."

I kissed him soft on the cheek and set my head back on the pillow.

The next morning after Billy left for the fields I didn't put my hair up the way I usually did. I sat down in front of the looking glass and combed it out real good. Then I put on the lipstick and cheek-rouge Momma gave me.

I didn't get up. I just sat there in front of the looking glass. It was like as if I hadn't really looked at myself for a long time, was looking at someone who'd grown to be almost a stranger. There was something different about the face that stared back at me. Then I reckoned the differing. It wasn't the face of a girl anymore.

All you got to do is let him see your charms, I told myself. He's a man, a man's yearnings will take care of the what-after. I remembered three years ago when Billy had brought Sam for Daddy to shoe. I'd been helping Momma pin the clothes on the line when he came down the road. There was something the matter with his leg, nothing too bad but enough so it was the first thing you noticed of him.

Then as he got closer I saw the brown hair and gray eyes, the sun-browned face, high-boned and handsome. I saw the strength in his arms, the muscles that wrapped around his bones like muscadine vines. It was like his upper portion and his legs belonged to two different bodies. You could tell those arms and shoulders was able for more heavy sweat than many another man's.

Yet there'd been a gentleness about him too. You could see it in the way he treated his horse. I wondered even then if the limp had somehow made him more kind and openhearted, the same way it had Matthew.

"I'll hang the rest of the clothes, Momma," I'd said.

Momma had looked Billy's way.

"I see," Momma said, giving me a little smile before walking back to the house.

Billy's eyes had been on me as well, from the moment he'd stepped in the yard. I was barely fifteen and for the first time in my life I knew what it felt to have a man honing me. There was something wanting and needful in his eyes, like I was a lacking part of himself that he didn't know was lacking till the moment he saw me. I knew it was something more than I felt for him, more than maybe I could ever feel for him or any another man.

"That man's taken quite a shine to you," Daddy had said after Billy left, telling me nothing Billy's blushes hadn't already made clear. I'd had never a doubt he'd be back to court and marry me.

I stared in the looking glass, into the blue eyes Billy saw that day when he'd showed up at our farm. I saw the lips I pressed against his that first night weeks later as we sat on the porch after Momma and Daddy and my brothers and sisters finally went in the house. I saw the yellow hair I took down on our wedding night when I got ready to lay with him for the first time.

I sat a while longer. Holland's hammer started up again, ever so close and persistent now. I fussed with my hair a bit more but I was just wanting to slow down what was going to happen.

I picked up my scrub-cloth and towel and walked out the front door into a spring morning all cool and bright. Dogwood blossoms bloomed full now and the branches looked like a skiff of snow laid on them. Oaks and poplars was springing green. You could almost hear them humming with new life. The sapling I'd planted yesterday looked to be holding its own. It needed watering but that could wait till later.

I looked across the plowed land and saw Billy in the cabbage next to the river, so far away he looked no bigger than a poppit-doll. I turned and walked around the house to the well, my eyes studying the ground. I wasn't going to flirt with him, not with words at least. If I was to have my way about it, there'd not be a word spoke between us. The hammer stopped for a few seconds. I knew Holland had his eyes on me as I crossed the back yard.

The hammering started up again but in a half-thoughted sort of way. I laid the towel and scrub-cloth and soap on the well and brought up pails of water and filled the wash tub. My back was to Holland when I started unbuttoning my dress but I could feel his eyes boring in on me. I heisted the dress over my head and laid it beside the towel. I picked up the soap and scrub-cloth. I eased myself into the tub with my back to Holland. The sun hadn't enough time to warm the water and goose bumps sprouted sudden on me like pebble-rocks.

I soaped up the scrub-cloth and rubbed it on my face and then my arms. The hammer was silent now. Everything was, like the woods too was waiting for what was going to happen. I listened for his footsteps but heard none. I washed my legs and then between them and finally my belly and my bosoms. My teeth chattered and my teats got hard and round like uncooked peas.

I stood up, faced myself toward Holland and stepped out of the tub. His dark-brown eyes laid full upon me, moving up and down my nakedness like as if it was something he was afraid he'd forget if he didn't study on it careful. I turned to pick up my towel. I heard him stepping toward me, stepping fast. I took a deep breath and then his arms laid firm on my shoulders. I knew then it had all been decided.

He didn't shove me to the ground or turn me to him or push me against the well. He wrapped his arms around my shoulders. It was me that turned to him. Holland had been working without no shirt on. His flesh felt warming against mine and I leaned against him longer than I ought have just taking in his heat. He tried to kiss me but I turned my face.

I stepped away and laid my towel on the grass, then my own self. Holland unloosed his overalls and laid down too, leaning his body onto me and then pushing himself inside, his beard all bristly against my cheek. I put my hands on his back and pulled him closer but I carried my mind as far in the way-off as I could.

I closed my eyes and went back years to quilt-washing day, recollecting how once a year in the spring Daddy and Momma would pile the quilts and washing powders and pails and the wash pot and all us young ones into the back of our pickup and we'd bump down the dirt road to the Whitewater River.

"You all go fetch some dry wood," Momma would say. "Me and your daddy will empty the truck."

We'd fill up our arms and take it back to where Daddy built his fire. All the while Momma filled the pot with pails full of river water.

When the water got hot and bubbling and Momma had dropped a washing powder in, Daddy took a big stick and doused the first quilt. He chunked the quilt to keep it under, then a ways later him and Momma both used sticks to haul it between them to the shallows.

Me and Ginny did the rest. We carried the quilts out to where the river was most to our belly buttons and swished and twisted the quilts clean. The current would be strong against us. We'd dig our feet into the white sand to hold our balance. It was a good, pure feeling to be out in the river on a warm spring day, knowing that come cold weather months later you'd lift quilts up to your chin and smell the washing powders and the damp of the river. But it was more than that. It was knowing something could be made clean no matter how soiled and dirty it got.

"That was nice and pleasuring," Holland said when he'd finished. He spoke his words in a soft sort of way and that was bothersome to me.

"You best get back to your fence-making," I said.

His brown eyes stared into my eyes, puzzled-like.

"Yeah," he finally said, and his voice sounded a little cross with me. "I reckon I better."

I pushed my hands against his chest and he rolled off. I got up and swaddled the towel around me. Holland still laid on the ground, like he hoped I might change my mind and lay back down with him.

"Momma told me your name but that was before I laid eyes on you," Holland said. "I'd of not forgot it if I'd reckoned on how pretty you was."

"You don't need to take any notice of my name," I said.

"I'll learn it again," Holland said, "and this time I'll not forget."

I picked up my dress and scrub cloth and went inside without another glimsen his way. I sat down in front of the looking glass with my brush and scrub cloth. I combed my hair to get the trash and tangles out, then rubbed the lipstick off my lips as Holland's hammer started up. I looked careful at myself, like I'd find some kind of stain or mark on my skin that hadn't been there a hour ago. But there wasn't any such a stain or mark. Nothing changes but on the inside, I told myself.

I got dressed and busied myself cooking a good noon-dinner for Billy. I tried not to ponder how long it had been since Billy had turned toward me in bed or how hard it had been to think of quilt-washing when Holland pressed his body against mine.

~

Holland came calling the next morning, dressed handsome in his soldier uniform like we was going to Seneca to the picture show. He had his hair roached back and shiny with oil, his breath sweet-smelling like cloves. I pulled a quilt off my line and laid it on the ground between us. I laid myself on it and hitched up my dress with never a word.

"There ain't no necessary in hurrying it," Holland said, laying down beside me. "Some things ought to be done in a easeful kind of way."

Holland laid his hand on my bosom and my teat budded to his touch.

Don't do that. Those were the words I should have said but my words melted like butter on my tongue as his hand moved soft over me like he was gentling a newborn. It wasn't no morning chill that made me shiver then or later when he unbuttoned the front of my dress.

"I've had women before but this here is different," Holland said later when he belted his pants.

"No, it ain't," I said, buttoning my dress. "It's the same thing, excepting this time you didn't have to pay."

That was a spiteful enough thing to say but I wasn't ever so certain whether I was spiting him or my own self.

"There's been women what didn't want my money," Holland said. "Two vowed they loved me. I had feelings for them too. I'll not deny that. But I never felt a yearning like I feel for you."

"I got chores to do," I said and started to lean myself up.

Holland's hand gripped my wrist. It wasn't no bruising grip but sure enough not to let me leave less he allowed it.

"I ain't trifling with you," Holland said. "I done some wrong things in my life but I ain't never been a liar."

"Let me go, Holland," I said, but I said it in a gentling sort of way.

Holland's fingers loosed my wrist.

"I'd never hurt you," he said.

~

Holland came back that afternoon and the next day and the day come after, always sweet-breathed and in his uniform, like we was sparking. Morning and afternoon I'd lay down with him on the quilt back of the house or in the woods or in the barn, anywhere but me and Billy's bed. He'd want to tarry and talk after but I wouldn't abide it. He'd try to kiss me and I'd turn my face. But that was near about all I didn't allow him. He did things to me Billy never had, things I'd never reckoned a man would know to do to a woman.

Then it was Sunday and me and Billy went to church. Holland wasn't there but his momma was. She glared my way with narrow eyes. It was easy enough to see she knew the truth of me and her boy but she could no more stop what was happening than she could stop the sun from rising.

On Monday morning Holland met me in the side woods next to the fence.

"I brung you something," he said, and reached me a war medal in the palm of his right hand. "It's a Gold Star. They gave it to me in Korea."

"I don't want nothing of yours," I said.

"You certain enough want one thing from me. You want it bad as any woman I ever been with." He closed his hand over the Gold Star. "I don't understand your ways," he said.

"You don't need too," I said and unbuckled his belt.

We laid down together then, his hand still closed around the medal. He was soon enough inside me. I turned my head so he couldn't kiss me. I looked toward the river and saw Billy in the distance. I remembered the first night Billy and I had laid down together, how it had hurt some but there was still a pleasingness in making ourselves one flesh. I remembered how the times after was better as the hurt disappeared.

Holland gasped. His mouth clamped on my neck and it seemed he was trying to suck the marrow out of me. His left hand tightened around my hair. Then I felt something else, something deep inside of me, a kind of brightness welling up and spreading all through my body like spring water when it bubbles out of the ground. At that moment I knew certain as anything ever in my life that Holland's seed had took root inside me.

We got up and picked the woods off our clothes. Holland opened his right hand and blood slicked his palm where the points of the Gold Star had jabbed through. He held his hand out like me seeing his blood on that Gold Star would change my mind.

"Like I done said, I want you to have it."

I shooed his hand away like the medal was no more than a bothersome fly.

"We'll never do this again," I said. "So don't come round no more."

He looked at me, his brown eyes searching mine for something he wanted to find in them. I turned away. I half expected him to grab at me, maybe slap me or call me a nasty name. I hoped he would but he didn't. For a minute he stood there still as a scarecrow as I walked to the house.

I'd just closed the door when I heard Holland come up the steps. His fist pounded the wood hard enough to shudder the whole house. I cracked the door a few inches but not before I fastened the latch.

"I want to marry you," Holland said.

"I got a husband, a good man I wronged being with you."

"I can be a good man. I'll quit my roughhousing. I'll treat you in a everloving way. You got my word on that."

"No," I said. "It's done over and finished between us."

"So you're just going to get shut of me."

For the first time I heard the fury in Holland. He seemed ready to tear that door right off the hinge and come after me.

"I'd kill any man done me like this."

"Don't darken this door never no more," I said.

Hit me, Holland, I thought. Hit me and make me lose what I can't help myself feeling. But the fury had sluiced out of him sudden as it rose. What was left in his brown eyes made me look down at the floor.

"You leave now," I said and he did.

The worse part's all done with and over now, I told myself as I leaned against the door, my heart pounding quick as a rabbit's.

Yet of course it wasn't and I was ever a foolish girl to think it was.

Billy couldn't help but see the mark on my neck and he let me know in a roundabout way he'd sighted Holland up here at least once. Billy didn't say anything else though it was clear he had his suspicions. He must have had more when I throwed up a few times a month later, or when I went to bed earlier, got tireder quicker as the last blossoms fell off the dogwoods and cicadas started singing in the trees. I'd see Holland in his fields every now and again but he kept his distance. He's forgot all about me, I told myself. He's certain for sure sparking some gal in Salem or Seneca, sweet-talking her the same way he did me.

All the while Billy didn't say the first thing about the throwing up and my tiredness, like as if it couldn't really be true without he made notice of it with his words, that silence could hide most anything between two people.

But come the dog days my belly poked out between us. There was no way to pretend any longer. The women at church had already figured it out by then and in little ways let me know as much.

"Whose child is it?" Billy finally asked.

As I answered that question I reckoned something I'd hid from myself for a couple of months—that all and everything had been headed toward this one moment where me and Billy would decide to go the rest of the way together or apart. It was like we'd been sick and failing and swallowed a draught that would cure or kill us.

The next morning Billy harnessed Sam and went to the field. The groundhogs had been bad to bother the cabbage so he took his shotgun with him. If he hadn't things might have went down a different path. Maybe not. Maybe there was but one path to follow from the moment I laid down with Holland.

I busied myself around the house a while before deciding to feed the chickens. When I stepped out on the porch Holland stood in the front yard by my dogwood sapling, standing there in his soldier uniform like I'd planted him there.

"It took me a while but when Momma told me you was in a family way I figured why you laid down with me," Holland said. "I know that's my baby inside you."

Holland strided across the yard and stepped up on the porch. He held his arms out to hug me. I stepped back, slapping at his arms as he pressed close.

"I'm part of you now and you're part of me," he said. "There ain't no other way about it and that baby will forever make it so."

Holland reached into his pocket.

"Here," he said, holding the Gold Star out to me. "You keep this for that young one."

That Gold Star laid in his palm like it was being weighted on a scale.

"A gift to that baby from his daddy," Holland said.

"I'll not take it," I said.

I slapped at Holland's hand and the Gold Star clattered against the porch wood.

"I can take care of you and that young one better than Billy can," Holland said. "I got more land. I got electricity. You come live with me."

"No, Holland," I said and backed up till I bumped the railing.

"I'd be a good daddy to that baby," Holland said. "I'll be a good husband to you." Holland reached his hand to hold mine.

A gunshot came from the field, no louder than the sound of Holland's hammer that first afternoon but enough to stop Holland, make him step off the porch to meet Billy under the white oak.

I stepped off the porch too. Soon enough Holland and Billy stood face to face. Billy had the shotgun but it was Holland doing all the talking.

"Please," I said, but whether my word was spoke to Holland or Billy I couldn't certain say.

Then the shotgun went off and my word or any another mattered not a whit.

Holland stumbled backwards, smoke wisping out of his chest like his heart was a fire that had been doused. The baby kicked hard inside me and I had no want to ponder that portent. I ran over to see how bad it was and saw Holland's face gone white as August cotton bolls. Hopeless as it was I'd of kneeled down beside him but for the way Billy's eyes had honed on me like it wouldn't much matter to him to mash that trigger again. Him and me just stood there, quiet as Holland who laid there dead between us.

It was like that shotgun had blasted all three of us outside of time, because the world of a sudden turned still and everlasting, and me and Billy and Holland was forever trapped, like weevils smothered in tree sap.

After a while me and Billy passed some words but there wasn't the least comfort in them. Then Billy went to the shed and got rope and a loop of barbed wire. He heisted Holland's body up on Sam and headed toward the river. I reckoned I knew what the end of that trip was.

"Things ain't never bad as they seem," Momma had always said in the worst times.

I spoke those words out loud but it did not a speck of good. I went inside and sat down at the table but after a while I picked up a rag and started dusting the front room, needful to give my hands something to do besides tremble. I ran my cloth across the fire-board but when I picked up the clock it slipped from my hand and hit the floor. The glass wasn't broke but the hands was on top of each other like dead man's hands and they was every bit as still. Just be ever thankful that glass ain't broke, I thought, for broke glass is the most bad luck there is. I laid the cloth down and went outside, figuring there'd be less things that could be tore up in the yard. I scattered cracked corn for the chickens, then got me some water from the well.

I was headed back to the house when I heard a shotgun blast down by the river. My knees got saggy and the water pail felt heavy as my heart. I laid the pail on the ground and steadied myself over to the porch steps.

All of everything bad roamed through my mind. Maybe Holland hadn't been dead. Maybe he'd got the shotgun and killed Billy. Carolina Power men had been up and down the river all summer. Maybe Billy had shot one of them too.

But my most worse thought was the sure likeliest, that Billy had leveled that gun on himself.

I sat there on the porch and waited, for it was all there was to do. If the worst had happened I'd soon enough see Sam, making his way back to the barn, maybe with Holland still strapped on his back. I closed my eyes. Let this all be a dream, I told myself. Let me wake up in my bed and all this just be imaginings.

It seemed a whole year passed before I saw someone coming up the riverbank. He stepped into the cabbage and picked up a hoe. I knew then it was Billy. I was going to go to him, tell how scared I'd been with all the bad thoughts loose in my mind but I knew he wouldn't want me down there. I watched him chopping the cabbage and knew what he was saying to me without the bother of words. Go on with your chores, Amy, each lift of his hoe said, act like nothing ain't happened.

I leaned myself off the steps to go inside and start a noon-dinner I had no craving for. That's when I saw the Gold Star, shiny on the gray boards like a piece of mica. I knew I had to hide it but not in the house. I crossed through the barbed wire Holland had strung and found a stump with a rot-hole. I laid the Gold Star inside. Even if it was to be found it'd be on Winchester land, not ours.

Billy stayed in the fields till suppertime. When he came in the furrows in his brow looked to be cut deeper. His gray eyes looked washed out and empty, the white of them red-veined like he hadn't slept for months.

I hugged him a long time. It was something he must have needed much as me for he wasn't the least wanting to let go. It was easy to reckon the why of that. Like me he'd had a mess of bad imaginings trailing him all day.

It was good for the both of us to hold onto something real, something we hadn't to be afraid of, because Billy was Billy again, not the man who'd killed Holland or the man who'd talked scowlful at me. We went on inside and sat down to supper but neither of us had any hunger though we'd had not a crumb since breakfast.

"I had to shoot Sam," he said. "If anybody asks, tell them he broke his leg."

Billy's eyes wandered out the window, then come back to mine.

"Sheriff Alexander gave me a little visit."

When Billy said that I got weak and trembly again for I hadn't figured that part of it would be on us so hasty.

"He'll be back and he'll certain sure have some words with you," Billy said. "If he asks about Holland, you or me didn't see him at all today and he ain't been over here the last few months. We're going to go about it like nothing happened."

Billy gentled his words, but there was iron in his eyes.

"You understand?"

I nodded.

"And you ain't never going to tell me what you did with Holland?"

"It's one less thing you have to act out not to know," Billy said.

There was no doubting the smarts behind Billy's words, for there'd be plenty enough else for me to lie about. I looked at Billy and wondered how after all that had happened this day we could sit down to supper and act like things was no different than any another evening. But the how of that was easy enough answered. A time such as this was when you most had to do such a thing, for it was the most common things that might could get you through.

I recollected what Momma did when my Uncle Roy got killed in the World War. She'd been on the porch that morning with a peck basket of pole beans and a big gray-metal wash tub when my Uncle Wade came to the farm to tell her. Momma had laid her chin on her chest. You could see the tears dripping into that big wash tub but all the while she kept stringing and snapping beans. She hadn't quit till every one of those pole beans was inside a mason jar.

As I thought of that morning years ago I reckoned how shameful it was to argue me and Momma being the same. Momma did no wrong to profit that kind of misery but I did plenty to bring about mine.

"I'll start on a baby crib tomorrow," Billy said, getting us both back out of ourselves. "You best lay down for a while," he said. "You and that baby need some rest."

"I reckon I will," I said and got up, leaving the dishes and pots where they laid for it hit me of a sudden how wore out I was, like I'd had so much worrying up to that moment I hadn't had a chance to take notice.

I laid down without a hope of sleep for my mind was busy as a bee hive. I kept seeing that smoke coming out of Holland's chest. I kept hearing what Holland said to me on the porch.

The sun dipped behind Sassafras Mountain after a while. The last light drained from the window but all that meant was I didn't no longer need shut my eyes to see Holland there on the ground dead.

When Billy came to bed he nuzzled up close for the first time in ever a long while. He laid his hand flat on my belly and there was comfort in knowing he wanted to feel the baby stir. It was a way of telling me that whatever happened we'd all three be a family.

Good a husband as he's been to you, how could you have ever had feelings for another, I said to myself. I wanted us to hold each other so I turned, not sure of what he might do.

But his wanting was strong as mine. We rubbed our bodies together in the dark and it was better than any time other. It was like all that had happened in the last few months, all that had happened today, had got us to where nothing could ever more be hidden between us. I held him tight and pushed his body against mine and soon me and Billy was moving together in a way we never had before.

"Just lay there and let him have his way," Momma had told me the day before I married, like it was a shameful thing for a woman to show a man how to pleasure her body. I was beyond such notions as that now.

"Keep doing it, Billy," I said. "It feels so good when you're in me."

We did other things, things I'd never have reckoned to have done with Billy even in the dark. It was like I was opening up more and more to him, showing him everything there was of me, our bodies swirled together like two creeks becoming one. But all the while I kept my eyes wide open, let the moonlight that spilled on the bed show me Billy's body, Billy's face. I was afraid to shut my eyes, afraid if I did it would be Holland's body tangled with mine, Holland's breath hot against my ear.

Soon enough we was breathing fast, touching and kissing in a heavy-fevered sort of way. Then it was like as if my body was nothing but water spreading out into the dark, each ripple taking me farther and farther away from all that burdened me. I came back to myself slow, slow enough for to fall asleep.

~

After the day Holland got shot, that baby was persistent in letting me know it was inside of me. It fussed and kicked most any hour like it was afraid I'd forget it was there. The more real that baby was inside me the more everything else seemed trifles. Even the law searching every nook and cranny of the farm didn't heavy my mind much as it ought have. September came. Things I would have made much notice of any another fall—how beech trees turned shiny bright like they was filled with goldfinches, or how maple leaves favored red stars, hardly caught my eye.

At church Mrs. Winchester spoke not a word to me or Billy but her eyes was steady on us. The other people in church couldn't help but notice. They knew what Mrs. Winchester claimed about me and Billy.

"Don't pay her no mind," Momma said. "That no-account son of hers has run off and left her all alone. She's addled with grief."

"She's a sour old woman who'd blame any but her own self for her troubles," Ginny said. "And I've a mind to tell her so."

It was in October Momma and Ginny had my baby shower one Sunday after church.

"Here," Momma said, handing me the first cup of cider she poured. "This will keep that young one warm."

The other women soon gathered round me.

"You be sure to carry a bloodstone in your left pocket these next few months," Edna Rodgers said.

"And don't look at no cross-eyed woman or eat strawberries," Martha Whitmire added.

A half-dozen others had their say before Sue Burrell took me by the arm.

"You don't need to be standing long either," she said, making me set down on the front pew.

Most of what the older women was telling me was just so much silliness but I made a show of listening. I knew it was their way of letting me know I shared something ever so wondrous with them, something you couldn't make words for so you talked around it with advice and old wives' tales.

We passed a good hour talking and sipping the cider. Ginny cut the pound cake she'd made and reached me a piece like I couldn't stand up and get it myself.

"Do you need some more cider, honey? Maybe some more cake?" someone would ask every few minutes, making a fuss over me.

It wasn't till I started unwrapping my gifts that the church got sudden quiet.

"I didn't invite her," Momma said softly.

I followed Momma's eyes to the back of the church. Mrs.

Winchester closed the door and walked down the aisle. She had a gift in her hands. The other women stepped aside and let her stand in front of me.

She locked those dark eyes steady on me. I reckoned she knew some things, things she hadn't told Sheriff Alexander.

"For the baby," she finally said and laid the box on my lap.

Then she went on out the door without never another word to any of us. I looked at the gift, the white tissue paper that covered the box, the blue bow tied around it. That box was light as a moth but I felt so sudden weak I was afraid to try and lift it.

"Leave me have that," Momma said, raising it off my lap. She laid it at the far end of the pew.

"Here," Ginny said, reaching me a smaller package. "Open this one. It's from Laura Alexander."

I didn't open Mrs. Winchester's gift till I got back to the house. I sat down in front of the fire, my hands all trembly as I tore off the bow and paper. I opened the box and there was Holland's face staring at me. He was seventeen, maybe eighteen, and dressed in a dark suit, a suit a man might wear to his wedding or be buried in. I pondered that picture longer than I ought have, knowing how easy a thing it would be to squirrel it away somewheres Billy would have no leave to look. But I didn't do that. I laid the picture in the fire and watched it curl up and turn black.

As I watched that picture turn to ash, I recollected my promise to Widow Glendower and my thoughts of Holland whittled away most to nothing for there was a fear now in my mind that hadn't been even when Sheriff Alexander and his men was thick as gnats all over the farm. Whatever else the law might do to me and Billy, they wasn't going to hurt my baby. But Widow Glendower could.

My mind turned back to a story Grandma had told around the fire, a story about a witch over in Long Creek that burned a newborn for power the doing of such a thing gave her. The witch had raked up the baby's ashes and bones to make charms and potions. That witch had caught that baby, pulled it right out of its momma and cut the biblical cord. Soon as that was done the witch let that momma bleed to death in the birth-bed while she toted the young one into the woods and built a fire. I could no more shake that story out of my mind than a hound could shake off a tick.

"I figure Widow Glendower to be your granny-woman," Ginny said the next week, like there wasn't a doubt in the matter.

"No, I asked Ella Addis," I said.

"I wouldn't if it was me," Ginny said. "The Widow has saw it all. There ain't many a fix she couldn't find the way out of to save a momma and her baby. Besides, she's near two miles closer than Ella Addis. What if that baby comes of a sudden?"

"I made up my mind, Ginny," I said. "You might as well be talking to a fence post for the hope of changing it."

Little as Widow Glendower gets out of that hollow, she won't know, I told myself most every waking hour. That's how I tried to soothe myself but in my heart I reckoned sure as the sun rising Widow Glendower would know when my baby came. She'd know the very second and there'd be plenty a price to pay for not keeping my part of the bargain. For the first time since the night after Holland had been killed, I had trouble sleeping. I dreamed constant of babies and fire.

~

The birth pains came on me at the end of January. Nature makes you lose the memory of the bad hurt it is to have a young one, the old women claimed, else you'd never have but one baby. I soon enough understood the so-true of that. Billy had been ailing since November, sniffling and coughing. He was only the least better off than me but he got in the truck and drove to get Momma and Ella Addis.

It seemed more than forever before he got back. The pains got worse and the floor swagged under me each time they came. I found my way to the bed and laid down. My insides felt to be seizing up like a giant hand had me round my middle.

I closed my eyes and tried to think of pleasant things, like the purple rhododendron blossoming on Colt Ridge in June, of how comforting it felt when Billy laid his hand on my stomach while we slept. I tried to think how by tomorrow I'd be holding the young one in my arms and this would all be just a remembering. Thinking such things helped some in the between but when the pains came they flooded everything out of my mind but the hurting.

When I finally heard the truck I liked to have cried I was so eased. Ella Addis came bustling through the door wearing her white apron and bonnet, the black doctoring bag in her hand. Momma was a step behind, looking fretful when she saw me laid out on the bed. Ella pressed her hand on my pooched-out belly like she was feeling a pumpkin to certain it was ripe. She poked me a little then seemed satisfied.

"It hurts," I said.

"Of course it does, honey," Ella said. "Nothing that's born is born without suffering. That's a big boy baby you're carrying and you're a smallish woman."

She patted my hand.

"You'll be all right. It's turned the right way. It's getting ready for old Ella to catch it."

Ella spread a clean white cloth on the table by the bed. She got out her scissors and needle and thread, then her salves and eye drops for the baby's eyes.

"You know all the what-else that needs to be done," Ella told Momma. "So you best get to it."

The next pain riffled through me and I couldn't help but moan. That brung Billy to the bedside. He looked frayed and weary but some scared was in him too.

"Here," Ella said and put a rag to my mouth. "Chomp down on it when the worst is on you."

"You go on," she said to Billy. "A man can't do nothing but get in the way at such a time as this, especially one looking puny as you. Go make yourself a pallet and lay down."

Billy did what he was told. The next pain came and it was worse. I chomped the rag but I couldn't feel any good of it. I shut my eyes and the pain was on me so bad it was near like I could see it, like it was a color and that color wasn't yellow or orange but the white you'll see in a lantern flame, a flame hotter than any other.

I poured sweat now and thrashed about the bed like as if I was having a bad dream. Momma was soon back beside me and held my hand and talked soothing while Ella gripped my legs till she stilled them. Then she reached into her apron pocket and brought out her snuff tin.

She took a pinch of snuff and stuck it under my nose.

"Sniff that, girl," she said.

I did what she asked and took a sneezing fit.

"Good, good," Ella said. "That'll help it along."

The hurting came again. I jerked my head to the side like I could turn away from that pain. When it finally passed I opened my eyes facing the window. It was the shank of evening now and what sun there'd been during the day now mostly fell behind Sassafras Mountain. Last night's snow still covered the ground and the snow and last light had the deepest indigo blue kind of color about them. I notioned it was the way the ocean bottom must look. Still as the ocean bottom too for there wasn't a breath of wind.

Then I saw Widow Glendower and Mrs. Winchester standing under the white oak where Billy had killed Holland. Or at least I reckoned I saw them for another pain came and my eyes squeezed shut despite myself.

I spit the rag from my mouth when the pain eased.

"They're out there," I told Momma and jerked my head toward the window. "Out by the white oak."

Momma peered through the window.

"There ain't nobody out there, Amy," Momma said. "You just ease your mind on that, honey."

I looked out the window and saw Momma was right. There wasn't no one out there, at least not anymore.

"That young one's ready to show himself," Ella said. "You mind to that and start pushing."

I did what she said and that white flame of pain laid down on me ever more than before.

"Its head is coming," Ella said and the pain was steady now. Momma reached the rag back in my mouth and squeezed my hand.

"Push, girl," Ella said. "His head's peeking out."

I loosed my hand from Momma and grabbed my hands against the back of the mattress. I leaned up on my elbows and saw Ella with her hands out to catch the baby. I pushed and felt my body tear open and it was like I could hear it the way you'd hear a sheet being ripped. I saw what had been inside me slide into Ella's hands and knew right then nothing so bloody and drowned-looking could be alive.

In that second I knew my punishment was to have my baby be born dead and I was hoping I'd die right then and there as well. Then it gave out a big wail. Ella reached the baby to Momma and picked up the scissors and cut the biblical cord. He wailed out some more when Ella put the drops in his eyes.

"You clean him off," Ella told Momma. "I got to sew this girl up."

I saw Ella reach for the needle and black thread and laid back down. I felt the needle and thread pushing through my skin but after what I'd just been through it was no more troubling than a sweatbee sting. I was more tireder than ever I'd been in my life, wore down beyond weariness. But I had to be sure of things before I could rest.

"Nothing's the matter with him, is there?" I asked.

"He's fine," Momma said, "as handsome a baby as ever I've seen."

"Bring him to me, Momma," I said, so she laid him on my stomach. I looked into his eyes and searched his face careful for any marking. I raveled loose the blanket and counted his fingers and toes.

"See if he'll nurse," Ella said.

Momma helped lean me up on some pillows. It took a few minutes but soon enough he was drawing my milk. The happiness of it settled over me like sun after rain. I closed my eyes.

"Ten days before you let her out of bed," Ella Addis said to Momma.

"You hear me, girl?" Ella said, but her voice seemed too far away to bother with a answer.

For the next nine days it was like I never full woke up. I laid in bed while Momma bustled around the house doing the cooking and cleaning. She'd bring the baby to suckle and leave him till he got fussy or needed his diaper changed. Momma brought me my food and between meals had me drink hot tea made with the sang and yellow dock Ella Addis said I'd need to gain my strength back. The tea was a soothing thing, maybe as much the warmness flowing through me as anything. After I'd drink it I always drowsied off.

Billy did what he could to help, taking Daddy's truck down to Seneca to get things Momma told him we needed, making sure there was enough wood stacked on the porch. He came in to see me every few hours but Momma wouldn't let him near the baby or spend much time with me. She was worried we'd catch what Billy had. He slept on a pallet in the front room while Momma made hers next to my bed. At night I'd hear him coughing. Each morning when he came in to see me more of his color had left him. He was shucking weight too, for every time he tried to eat he'd take a coughing fit.

"We got to name that child," Momma said after a week.

"There's no good to come from that baby not having a name."

I'd been waiting for Billy to get spry again but the way he was looking that would be some while so I took out the Bible to give him a Godly name. I thought it might put him in God's favor to do that, put him in God's favor despite what his momma and daddy did to get and keep him. I settled on Isaac.

"That's a proud enough name for any boy," Momma said, and Billy made no argue against it either.

The tenth morning I got up from my birthing bed. My legs was a bit unsteady at first and I tottered around like a colt taking its first steps. It was like I'd forgotten how to walk but soon enough I was feeling like myself again. Momma still stayed with me during the day. Daddy picked her up after supper and didn't bring her back to mid-morning. She was letting me take my house back over but she was going to make sure I did it slow.

Isaac was a big baby and it seemed every morning I woke up and looked at him he'd gotten bigger.

"That's the growingest young one I ever seen," Momma said, "and not the least bit colicky."

Yet as the weeks passed by, the stouter Isaac got the punier Billy seemed. Billy was fevered now, his skin pale and clammy. He soon dragged his pallet in front of the fire. He swore he couldn't get warm though the sweat poured off him like rain. It seemed now that the baby was out of my belly it took strength from Billy the same way it once did from me.

I got Daddy to drive down to Seneca for Doctor Wilkins. Doctor Wilkins stuck a thermometer in Billy's throat and had to hold it there for Billy was so on the down-go he couldn't do it himself.

"Pneumonia," Doctor Wilkins said. He gave Billy a shot of penicillin and some big red pills to take twice a day.

"That should fix him up," Doctor Wilkins said. "You send for me if he's not doing better by Friday."

"There ain't nothing to fret about," Momma said. "Give him a couple days and he'll be frisky as a gray squirrel."

I nodded but I had my doubts. I reckoned I had a owing that was going to be paid one way if not another.

The shot didn't make Billy no better. The fever was constant on him now and it was starting to bother his mind. At night he'd point at shadows and swear someone was there and that someone was Holland. That put more scare into me than anything since the killing.

"I best send your daddy to fetch Doctor Wilkins," Momma said the second afternoon, but I was beyond believing in what Doctor Wilkins could do. There was but one person that could help Billy. I knew it certain sure I'd have to see her and soon if Billy was to stay out of the burying ground.

It had been flurrying off and on all day so I bundled up good. I filled the lantern with oil because I'd not get there before dark. I went into the back room and got the box of kitchen matches, then reached in the salt tin and poured a handful in my pocket.

"Where on earth do you think you're setting out for?" Momma asked.

"You stay with Billy and Isaac," I told Momma. "It's something that's got to be done."

"I'll not let you go out in such weather," Momma said, but I was already out the door. Isaac started squalling and Momma stood still with the door open, not sure who to go to, me or the baby.

"You come back here," she said, but I was in the yard now, the inch of snow under my feet making my steps soft and whispery. I heard the door shut and in a few seconds Isaac got quiet.

The wind blew steady and flurries stung my face. The sun was near snuffed out by the clouds that sagged down like a big gray quilt. I crossed the barbed wire fence onto Mrs. Winchester's land and found the stump. I grabbled down in the hole till I rooted up what I was searching for, then followed the fence to the river and then the trail upstream. I could tell all the bed laying had taken my wind from me. I was huffing and puffing and hadn't walked a half mile yet. I stopped to gain back my breath and remembered myself I'd at least be walking downhill on the way back.

The flurries got thicker till they was more than flurries and if there'd been a choice about it I'd have turned around. But I didn't believe there was no choice, at least as far as keeping Billy alive. Wind whipped up enough to bury the sound of the river. Light was hiding fast now and the only way to follow the trail was the gaps in the woods. Soon I could barely see my feet, much less the trees.

I knew if I strayed too far right I'd be in a bad fix for there was drop-offs where the trail nudged up close to the river. I stopped to pump the lantern and took out my box of kitchen matches. I had a time of it getting the lantern lit. The wind snuffed the matches quick as I struck them. One finally held long enough to catch the wick. I reached the lantern out before me but still had to step slow and certain for I could see no more than a few yards ahead.

It seemed long as forever before I got to where Wolf Creek ran into the river. Not far now, I told myself, and started into the hollow, full dark but for the lantern, the snow flying thick. It was slow going but I found my way till I came to where the big rocks squeezed the path tight. One of the big rocks had tumbled down and plugged up the gap like a cork in a bottle.

There was no way but to go around. I left the path and went up the left ridge. The land was sidling and snow slicked the ground. I tried to hold my balance but soon enough I slipped and slided down and down, bumping rocks and trees and getting a mouthful of snow. The lantern flung out of my hand halfway down and I heard glass shatter against a rock.

For a minute or two I just laid there on the snow and checked myself for broke bones. There wasn't any, though I knew I'd be purpled up good by morning, if I saw morning. I tried to get myself calmed down. You ain't too far from her house, I told myself, no more than a field's length away. But my notion of direction was lost in the tumble. Downhill, I told myself. You're up on a ridge. You go down and find the path. If you can't find the path, find the creek. It'll lead you the rest of the way.

That sounded easy enough except I had tumbled onto level ground. Every step I took in any direction a laurel branch slapped my face or tripped my feet. It was like some kind of monster with a thousand arms was grabbing at me. I was soon spun around so much as to not reckon if my feet and face was pointed in the same direction.

There was no moon or stars to follow and the wind had died down so as not to give me direction. The snow was just another thing confusing me. I was in the worst kind of fix for the cold had got on the inside of me when I took my tumble. I reckoned I'd not last if I had to wait out morning to see my way to help.

Then I remembered the kitchen matches. I reached down slow, almost afraid to know sure if they was still there, for they was the last smidgen of hope I had. I felt the box bulged in my pocket and I almost cried for the relief of it.

I struck one and got a glimsen of the laurel slick and stumbled a few feet in one direction. Then I struck another one and made my way a few more feet the same way. My fingers counted ten more matches but I saw no choice but to use them. I struck another and then another and I'd made it back into trees and where the land took a slanting.

I knew which way the creek was now but I was of a sudden weary and felt ready to just set down and get it over with. It was the cold doing that to me and I made myself mindful of things to make me go on. Think of your baby, I told myself. After all you done to be his momma, you ain't going to leave him without a momma. Think of your man too. He'll die if you do. I prayed then. There seemed no other way I'd get saved.

"Get me out of this fix, God," I prayed right out loud. "Don't do it for me. Do it for that innocent baby. Get me out of this so he can have parents to raise him."

I struck another match and made my way a few more steps. I struck another and saw the big rocks but I was on the other side above them now. I struck three more matches. I didn't find the path, had walked right across it without knowing, but I found the creek. I figured to be close now. I stepped right into the creek and walked up it, not caring that my shoes was getting doused. I fell a couple of times but got myself up and walked on.

Then all of a sudden water splayed out in two different directions. I took another step and my feet was on dry land and it was like the creek had disappeared under the ground.

I raised another match and saw the creek forked. I was standing on dry ground there between two prongs. At any another time I'd have known to follow the left fork but the cold had got so into my mind I couldn't think out the simplest thing. I just stood there between the two prongs, my body going numb and no idea which way to go.

Then something brushed against my left leg, something big. If I'd of had my full mind that might have finished me off. I'd have been near terrified to death it was a panther or a bear. But my mind wasn't working that way. I wasn't scared. I was just a little curious to what might be bothering at me.

I fumbled a match from the box and dropped it in the creek. That left me one. I steadied my hands best as I could and struck the last match and there beside me was the black dog I'd last seen in April. The dog nudged my hand and took a few steps up the left prong. The match went out but I followed the sound of him, more because it was easier than trying to think out anything else to do.

We hadn't gone but a few yards when I saw a square of light. I stumbled across the yard and up on the porch. I knocked on the door. Then I just slumped down on the porch and everything grew dark like as if a coffin lid had closed over me.

When I woke up I was warm. I opened my eyes to a big fire just a arm's length from where I laid. A pillow eased my head and quilts heaped heavy on me. A chair, the same chair I'd sat in last April, crowded close to the fire. My stockings and dress and overcoat laid on it.

"You've had yourself quite a adventure tonight."

I turned and saw Widow Glendower in a chair on the other side of my pallet. She was knitting, the balls of thread at her feet. The big needles caught the firelight and glimmered like silver.

"How long I been asleep?" I asked, my face still mashing the pillow.

"Oh a good long time, girl. It's near dawn."

That woke me up good for my first thought was if Billy had made it through the night. I got up and faced the fire as I put my dress and stockings on.

"So how's your young one?" Widow Glendower said.

Warm as I was it was like that old woman had laid a handful of snow on my heart. I turned to face her.

"My baby's fine," I said.

"I thought we had us a agreement."

"I was afraid you'd hurt him."

Widow Glendower gave a laugh.

"So you believe that slack talk about me after all. Is that why you got salt in your pocket?"

"Yes," I said, saying it bold for my mind was heavy with how Billy was faring.

"And what might be your reason for to visit me?" she said.

"My man's pining away with a fever."

"And you think I done that to him?"

"Yes," I said. "It's a way to get square with me for not letting you be my granny-woman."

"If I wanted to revenge you why didn't I let you freeze to death out on my porch?" Widow Glendower asked.

Because maybe you got the wanting of something more than just folks' lives, I thought.

Widow Glendower shuffled into the other room. She came back with a poke and went straight to the big blue trunk in the corner. She bent down and sorted out what she was looking for.

"Here," she said, laying the poke at my feet. "There's willow bark and boneset. Make him a tea of it and his fever will break."

"He'll live then?"

Widow Glendower didn't answer.

"You claim to see things that ain't yet been."

"I reckon I do," she said, like it was something she'd forgotten.

She looked into the fire. I recollected again what Grandma had said, that flames was the devil's tongue reaching up out of hell. If that was so I reckoned that tongue was speaking to Widow Glendower now.

"Fire and water," she finally said. "Fever's a fire. Your man's not to die by fire, leastways if you give him what's in that poke."

I looked out the window and saw the dark was drawing back. Snow had quit falling and everything looked quiet and still like a calendar picture. I fetched my shoes from under the chair and laced them up. Then I grabbled in the matchbox and pulled out the Gold Star.

"Here," I said. "I found it in the woods a few months ago. It looks to be pure gold. I reckon it ain't enough of what I owe but it's something."

I didn't know if she'd take it or not but she opened her palm.

I put on my coat and picked up the poke.

"I best be headed back home."

I stepped out on the porch and the dawning was milky-blue. The snow had hardened up and made a crunching sound every time I laid my foot down, but it wasn't slippery and I made my way down to the river without much bother. The rest of the way home was trifling easy for the sun was out bright by then.

When spring returned and the dogwoods lit up the woods, I tried not to think of all that began the last time they had bloomed. I could keep those rememberings off my mind days at a time for I was so busy tending to Isaac and my chores. Yet thoughts of those bad times laid deep in my mind like river snags. They would raise to the surface ever so often just to let me know they was still there. When they did I had never a doubt there'd come a time I'd pay for all that had happened and the cost would be a lot more than a piece of gold.

the Husband

WHEN deep summer comes and the Dog Star raises with the morning sun, the land can scab up and a man watch his spring crop wrinkle brown like something on fire. It's the season snakes go blind. Their eyeballs coat over like pearls and they get mean. A rattlesnake allows no warning and a milk snake that would have cut the dust to the tall grass in June quiles up and strikes at anything that steps its way. It's a time when foxes and dogs go mad. They'll come shackling toward you, their lips snarly and chins white with slobber. You'll raise your gun and they'll come on like they just want to get it done with.

Sometimes that time of year a man will act no different. A man who any another time would step around trouble, a man who, if his truth be known, might be a bit of a coward, will of a sudden turn mean and crazy. He'll do something nobody, even himself, would reckon likely. He'll even kill a man.

"You couldn't give me a child. I had to be with one that could," Amy said the first week of August when her stomach swelled like a muskmelon and neither of us could counterfeit any longer not to know.

By then that baby was about the only thing growing. Corn stalks stood dead in the fields, the beans half-buried in gray dust. The only crop that looked to make it was tobacco I'd planted beside the river, that and some cabbage, if the groundhogs didn't get it.

"Whose child is it?" I asked, like when I'd been down by the river that spring plowing I hadn't looked up to see Holland Winchester saunter past the big white oak that marked the property line between his family's land and mine, and like when I came back to eat my noon-dinner that day my beans and bread wasn't ready and Holland had left his mark on Amy, a spot on her neck purpled like a fox grape.

I waited for Amy to answer my question, my mind taking me back a month to the July afternoon I first suspicioned her being with child. The weather had turned summer by then so the wash tub was out back near the well. After supper Amy had got her towel and such and went to bathe while I took my whetstone out and sharpened my scythe. She'd drawed her water early afternoon so it'd be sunny-warm come evening. All she needed was to take off her clothes and get in.

When I'd got my scythe sharpened I tarried by the window and watched Amy bathe, because that was a sight so pretty as to make my heart ache, not so much in a lusting way but something somehow above that. A woman is never more pretty than when she's bathing or so it was when I looked at Amy. A man bathes just to get dirt off him but it seems more to a woman than that. Amy bathed in a slow, easeful way like the soap and water washed away every care the day had laid on her. Then she took the tin and sloshed water over her head and her yellow hair darkened to the color of honey.

The sun had been slaunchways over Sassafras Mountain so when Amy raised from the wash tub the water streamed off her like melting gold. There's no angel in heaven more lovely than this, I told myself. Then Amy turned as she stepped from the tub. I saw the curve of her belly, a curve no more than the scythe blade I held in my hand but enough to wonder me about her and Holland Winchester. I raised my finger to the blade and ran it across the edge. I felt the steel cut right through. Drops of blood bright like holly berries spotted the floor.

I hadn't wanted to follow that trail where Amy's ripening belly led. I tried for a month to keep what I suspicioned about Amy and Holland clear of my mind but it came creeping back when my thoughts got idle, the same way a rat waits for things to get all still and silent before it shows. I hadn't said the first word to her. I was scared to, scared as I'd been when I reckoned the polio would take my legs from me.

What really set the fear in me wasn't so much Amy carrying another man's baby but losing her to that other man, because in the years we'd been married she'd became a part of me ever sustaining as my legs. Even when I was in the fields and her up at the house, my thoughts was often upon her. I'd think of her in the house cooking or canning, knowing that though we was working apart we was still working for each other.

So all that July I hadn't offered a word to Amy about her belly. I'd known once it was words something would come of those words. If that something was losing Amy I'd be in a fix I couldn't see my way out of. I'd been like a man in his field who sights a tornado hauling towards him and puts his head down reckoning if he don't look up and admit to its coming it might some-ways pass him by.

But Amy's belly had just kept on waxing like the moon. Now as the Dog Star raised up with the morning sun, that tornado I'd closed my eyes to had sucked me up in it and I had no notion of where it would set me down. But I was about to find out on a August dog day when most everything that surrounded me had seemed to lay down to die.

"Whose child is it?" Amy said, repeating me as she raised her blue eyes to mine. "It's my child, Billy. But it can be ours if you want."

Her saying that gave me pause, because there's currents that run deep in a woman, too deep for a man to touch their bottom. I'd seen the look on Amy's face when her younger sister's children crawled into Amy's lap. I'd heard her in the kitchen singing the last few months when I came up from my field. Amy had always carried a pretty tune but there was a difference now, a kind of smile in her voice I'd never heard before. She hadn't been singing because of me or Holland Winchester. At least that's what I reckoned. But I had to know for sure.

"What about him?" I asked, not wanting to own up Holland's name, because if I did I'd bring his face and body back into the house and I'd see what I'd been hauling in my head for months now—Holland Winchester and Amy in the back room, their clothes half off, him between her legs like a plow in a furrow.

"What about him?" Amy said, repeating me again.

"You leaving me for him?" I asked, for now that we'd started it was best to go ahead and see how the land lay between us.

Amy looked at me, her blue eyes steady as a plumb line.

"No. I'm your wife, Billy, not Holland's."

I suppose that should of swaged me some but right then I didn't feel nothing like good. Every man must eat a peck of dirt before he dies, Daddy had once told me. I felt I was eating of it by the shovelful.

"When's the last time you saw him?"

"Two months ago," Amy said. "Soon as I was sure it took I told him not to come round no more."

"What'd he say to that?" I asked.

"He didn't say much. I told him certain it was over and done with."

"Does he know you got a baby coming?"

"No, that's not his concerning," Amy said. "What's happened

between me and him is finished but it ain't finished between us, without you want it to be. That child can be mine or it can be ours."

Amy lifted her hand and brushed back a strand of yellow hair that had fell over her eye.

"So what you going to do, Billy?" she asked.

At that moment I truly did not know. I knew what many another man might do. He'd raise his hand and slap Amy stout enough to lay her flat on the floor. Some would do worse. Then they'd walk out the door and never come back.

"Do you love me?" I finally said, my eyes steady on hers. That was my last question, the one that most mattered.

Amy's blue eyes looked tired, the way they'd been a lot the last couple of months, but she looked pretty, prettier than she'd ever looked, her bosoms and hips fuller, her skin bright and glowing like she'd bathed in a tub of sunshine.

"Yes," she said.

"You swear you'll never be with him again," I said.

"I've done told you that," Amy said.

"Swear it then," I said.

"I swear it," Amy said.

~

In bed that night I listened to the cicadas calling for rain. The window was open but the air laid on the night still and stale as stump water. I couldn't hear the river the way I could any other time of the year. It was easy to believe the dog days had sucked it dry as a snakeskin.

I laid with my chest pressed against Amy's back, my hand on her stomach. I could feel the baby stir under my palm. As I dozed on and off it seemed I was touching my own belly, the young one inside me, not Amy. I was thinking, the way I often had since seeing Doctor Wilkins, about what my life might could have been without the polio.

Doing that was like mashing your tongue on a sore tooth, something that only gave more pain but you couldn't keep from doing it.

My thoughts went back twenty years, to the morning when I'd stirred awake with my head hot and hurting and my legs not listening when I told them to stand me up. Momma had her fearings of what it was and sent Daddy on horseback to Seneca for Doctor Griffen. Momma stayed on her knees while me and her waited through a hard couple of hours.

"Please, God, don't take my onliest boy from me," Momma said over and over.

She was less than certain to do anything else, even give me a sip of water though my throat was parched as roasted chestnuts.

Doctor Griffen had finally bumped up through our pasture in his big Dodge car. He stepped in the house toting a black doctor's bag big enough to be a grip. He was old, his hands liver-spotted and shaky, but Momma confidenced him.

"Can you move your legs?" he asked.

"No sir," I said.

Doctor Griffen just nodded to that.

"I'm needful of some water," I said.

Doctor Griffen took the stethoscope from his bag.

"We'll get you something to drink in a minute, son."

He poked the stethoscope around my chest, his eyes closed shut and listening. Then he asked had my neck stiffed up. I had to nod because by then I had a thermometer sprouting in my lips. He put his hands on my legs, the softest hands I'd ever known for a man. He took out the thermometer and studied it. Then him and Momma went out on the porch a few minutes. I finally got my glass of water and was asleep quick as it took me to close my eyes.

When I woke Doctor Griffen was gone. Daddy was back, sitting in a dinner chair he'd drawed up to my bed. Him and Momma stayed in that chair every night and day minute for the next week, watching my breath the way Doctor Griffen had warned them to. Every morning Momma sat at the foot of the bed and rubbed my legs and feet.

I'd got healed slow but by Christmas I was back tending my chores. But my right leg lagged behind and never caught up.

"You make more notice of that leg than anybody else does, Billy," Momma said.

But I was still skittish about it, especially around girls.

Then the time came when the shorter leg, the polio too, no longer seemed worth fretting over. Part of it was Amy. She never made notice of my leg, maybe because she had a brother that limped. But it was more than that. By the time I'd met Amy I'd paid enough of the bank loan to finally call the twenty acres I'd bought from Joshua Winchester my own. That had been a big doing for me. The only land Daddy and my Uncle Joel could claim was what dirt they carried under their fingernails.

"I'm looking for to sell, not sharecrop," Joshua Winchester had said when I came to see him about that land.

"I ain't come about no sharecropping," I'd said and handed him the check the bank had made out for me.

He'd studied it close, as like he didn't quite believe it was all on the up and up.

"All right," he had finally said and stuffed the check in his overall pocket. "A Holcombe owning land," he'd said, then smiled. "You're getting above your raising, boy."

I'd cleared that twenty acres by myself but for Sam, me and that horse yanking up stumps stubborn to come out as back teeth. It had been a man's work. You couldn't call no one a cripple who'd done it and it was like it hadn't been till then I'd truly got out of that bed I'd laid in so many years ago with my neck stiff as a hoe handle, my legs useless to walk on as two sticks of kindling.

I remembered that first Sunday after Amy had made it known

all over the valley that it was me with the problem, not her. The women of the church all made a fuss over her but they had not a word for me. Their eyes was on me though, and those cold stares reminded me of some of the folks who'd showed up at the farm when the worst of the polio was upon me. They came into the room where I laid and counterfeited they was mournful but their eyes made notice otherwise. They'd looked at me like I was something in a county fair sideshow, something queer and hardly human.

Now as I laid in bed with Amy, I reckoned there was ways I'd never got up from that sick bed after all. Doctor Wilkins hadn't said it but he hadn't had to. That polio had gelded me.

~

At first light I eased my hand off Amy's belly and got out of bed quiet as I could. I got me a chunk of cornbread and stepped out on the porch. My eyes lit on the dogwood Amy had planted in the spring, its leaves brown like cured tobacco and no more alive than a iron stob.

A sign of certain bad luck, my Daddy would have claimed, and I recollected how as a chap I'd been schooled by older kin to step lively if you wanted to stay out of bad luck's way, because it was coming at you from all directions day and night, coming even in your dreams.

If you saw a new moon through the trees or a black cat crossed your path, it was always a sign of coming trouble, the same if you heard a screech owl or rooster at night or you killed a toad-frog or dreamed about near anything from crows to muddy water. And though there was things of good luck such as horseshoes and redbirds and planting your crops on Good Friday, they was reckoned pretty flimsy up against all the bad luck in the world.

"No good will come from such a sight as that," Grandma said when she saw a letter in a writing spider's web.

"There's a death coming soon," Uncle Joel said when he heard a whippoorwill before dark set in.

It had vexed me how the older folks always seemed to look for the worst. I'd sworn myself not to do such the same when I grew up but it was coming clear to me now that it all hadn't been just silly notions. My kinfolks had crosshaired in on the truth of the world.

I thought of the luck I'd had the last few months, how in the first week of June my truck ran hot and when I checked my oil it came out white as milk. I knew right then my engine block had cracked and I'd not be able to fix it without I'd sold my crop. I recollected how the Dog Star showed early this year, just weeks after I put the truck in the barn. That had been more certain trouble.

And now Holland. If I'd had the want, I could have found plenty of signs telling me trouble was coming. Those signs would of proved real as a rock or tree or anything else in the world.

I looked above Amy's dogwood and saw the Dog Star raising up with the sun. I knew Amy was wrong to ever figure some words would keep Holland from doing as he pleased. I recollected how in eighth grade we all had been cutting up in class and our teacher Mr. Pipkin picked out Holland to punish though he'd been at it no worse than the rest of us. Maybe it was because Holland was the biggest. Mr. Pipkin held up a roll of black electrician's tape and told Holland he was going to tape Holland's mouth shut. Holland was stout, six feet tall by then and a sure two hundred pounds but Mr. Pipkin was as tall and outweighted Holland to boot. Holland had stood beside his desk, his hands by his side, fisted and ready.

"You've no cause to punish me and not the others," Holland said.

"You come up here now, boy," Mr. Pipkin said to Holland.

"I'll not," Holland said. "You come on and put that tape on me if you reckon you can."

Mr. Pipkin had muttered some things but all he did in the end was put the tape back in his desk.

If Holland had lived in another county or even another valley, maybe we'd have been shut of him, but not with just some strands of barbed wire to keep us apart. Him and me and Amy was linked now like the Dog Star and the morning sun.

I hitched up Sam and led him down to the cabbage patch. I fetched the .12 gauge to take with me, keeping close to the woods. The groundhog must have spotted me anyway. The only notice of him was two more chewed-up cabbage.

I did find a blacksnake though, quiled like a whip in the middle of a row. The old folks claimed you could kill a blacksnake and lay it on a fence and it would bring rain. I flattened the blacksnake's head with the gun butt and did that very thing, letting its slick white belly catch the sun. But I felt bad soon as I did it. I knew I wasn't trying to bring rain. I did it for no more than I was feeling mean. It was something I could hurt that couldn't hurt me back.

I checked the tobacco and then me and Sam plowed the cabbage. I kept glancing up toward the house and come midmorning I saw what I'd been hoping not to see. Holland Winchester straddled the barbed wire fence beside the white oak and walked into the front yard, the same way he came in April when I'd sighted him from this very field. Even when Holland was having his way with another man's wife he was too proud to skulk around back like a hound stealing eggs from a hen-house. No, that wasn't ever his way of doing things.

Amy saw him coming too and stepped out on the porch. She tried to wave him back but he came up the steps anyway. He opened his arms to her but Amy stepped back, slapping at his hands.

Sam stamped his hoof and snorted, ready to work. I stood with the reins around my neck and hoped that Holland would go back over to his side of the fence and leave us alone, because unlike Holland I didn't know if I was a brave man. I'd gone down to Greenville and they'd turned me down, 4-F. I hadn't had my grit tested the way Holland had in Korea. I didn't know what I'd do if Koreans came screaming and running toward me, certain to kill me if I missed or my gun jammed. I didn't know if I could kill a man. What I did know was if Holland didn't leave something would have to be settled, one way or another.

Every time Holland moved toward Amy she stepped back but she was almost to the railing. I didn't reckon at all for Holland to hurt her. I was scared of something else. I walked over to the field's edge and picked up the .12 gauge. I aimed at the sky and mashed the trigger.

Holland turned and looked down over the shriveled corn and beans to where I stood with the gun still aimed at the sky while I fumbled in my overalls for another shell. I reloaded and grabbed Sam by the reins, not bothering to unhitch the collar and trace chains.

I led Sam straight toward the house, straight toward Holland Winchester. We stumbled across rows of cabbage and then through the beans and corn, the corn stalks rasping and snapping when me and Sam cleared a trail right through them, the plow twisting and grabbing behind like a anchor. My legs felt heavy, like I'd been walking miles. That was the fear weighting down on me.

Holland stepped off the porch and met me in the shade of the white oak, the boundary between what was his and what was mine. My hands was trembly as I raised the .12 gauge, the barrel wavering in the direction of his heart like a compass trying to find true north.

"I wronged you when I laid down with her but we're way up the path from right and wrong now," Holland said. "What's swelling her belly is mine, not yours."

I met his eyes, eyes dark as molasses. I didn't know the exact of what I hoped to find in those eyes, maybe a speckle of fear for the shotgun in my hand, maybe a speckle of pity. But whatever it was I looked for I didn't find in those dark eyes.

"Just leave us alone, Holland," I said, letting my finger find the trigger.

"I can't do that," Holland said, his eyes not even blinking when I clicked the safety off.

Amy stepped into the yard but I nodded her not to come no closer.

"I'm not some stud bull you can use then take back to another farm," Holland said to Amy. "That baby's as much mine as yours. You're saying it ain't so won't change ever a thing."

Holland stepped toward me then, reached out and grabbed the barrel. If he'd of wanted he could have jerked the shotgun right out of my hands.

"Here," he said, pushing the barrel against his chest. "I'd have killed a man who done to me what I done to you."

My hands jittered but Holland steadied the barrel against his chest.

"Settle it now one way or another, Holcombe," Holland Winchester said, "because this here is the only way to keep me from claiming what's mine."

The cicadas sang overhead. It seemed like they got louder each second that passed, so loud it was like they'd crawled inside my head. Sweat stung my eyes and I had no free hand to wipe it away. I squinched my eyes but it did no good.

"Please," Amy said, and I didn't know if she was talking to me or Holland.

The .12 gauge's butt slammed against my shoulder and Holland stumbled backwards. His hand slid off the foot of barrel he'd held like a drowning man letting go of a life rope. I raised my left hand and dabbed the sweat from my eyes and reloaded. Holland's brown eyes stared right at me but he was seeing something else. Maybe it was himself as a child, or in a foxhole in Korea, or tangled in one flesh with Amy. Maybe he saw all those things, one after another flashing in front of him like he was looking at calendars filled with pictures instead of months and years.

Holland steadied himself. For a moment he stood his ground, the way he did in Korea. I watched the life fade from Holland's eyes like a pail getting gloamy as it sinks into a well. You've just killed a man, I told myself.

Holland's knees buckled, a puff of dust raising around him when he hit the ground. Amy ran to where he laid. She looked down at him and then at me, her face scared for maybe she reckoned I'd put that other shell in the .12 gauge for her. Maybe if she'd kneeled down beside him and started crying I would have shot her. At that moment I was crazy as any slobbering dog or shedding snake. But Amy didn't kneel down. Her eyes was dry as the dust she stood on.

All of a sudden my arms and legs got to twitching, as like parts of me wanted to shake free from my body and take off in all different directions, away from the awful sight of Holland laying there with a big hole in his chest. Get a hold on yourself, I kept saying, saying it right out loud.

Finally the twitching stopped. Amy stood close by, not saying nothing for a while, like she was afraid her words would set me off to twitching again, like words was to me like water to a mad dog. I took my breaths slow and easeful, trying to clear my thinking of anything but getting air in and out of me. After a couple of minutes my breath near leveled out.

"What are you going to do?" Amy finally said, the same question she'd asked yesterday.

"I've got to study on it," I said, my voice calmer than I'd figured it to be. It was like the fit had shucked all the panic out of me, at least for a while. "I ain't going to the jailhouse if I can help it, and I ain't going to Texas or California. If I was going to tuck tail and run I'd of went yesterday."

Amy didn't say nothing to that. She looked at me like I was somebody she couldn't quite place. I was feeling a stranger to myself as well. It would take some while to get used to being a murderer.

"Get on in the house," I said, and I said it kind of bristly for bad thoughts came sudden to me, swirling around in my head like bats in a cave. Bad thoughts like maybe Amy had planned on Holland killing me instead of me killing him. Or even if I could have sired a child she'd of rathered Holland do it. I had a thought-picture of her and Holland in the back room, the bed shaking and squeaking underneath them, her hands on his back pushing him deeper into her.

"Go on," I said.

Amy had enough smarts to do what I told her.

I sat down on a root that raised out from the white oak like a half-buried leg. I laid my head on my knees and closed my eyes, shedding my mind of all the bad thoughts that kept trying to roost in my head.

When I opened my eyes, it was like waking up from a bad dream because nothing that had happened since I'd aimed the shotgun at the sky seemed real. But Holland Winchester's body was real and it was laying no more than a coffin-length from where I sat. The bluebottle flies and yellow jackets had already found him. The law would too by and by if I didn't soon do something.

Holland's truck would still be at his house. His momma would know he hadn't gone far. I wondered if she knew he was coming over here and the what-for of his visit. I reckoned Mrs. Winchester had her suspicions, especially since he was dressed more for sparking than farm work. I pondered if she'd heard the shot and already knew, the way a momma will sometimes know, that trouble had found her boy. For all I knew, she could have already telephoned the law.

I sure knew I couldn't bury him. A fresh-dug grave would be so easy a thing to find. Besides, hard as the ground was I'd still be digging when the law showed. I couldn't hide him neither for anything dead in the dog days gets rank in the worst sort of way.

The river was the natural place. I could take a big flat river rock and tie it to Holland's chest and sink him in a blue hole. But there'd be a trick to that since I could swim no better than a rock my own self. Even if I was slick enough to get it done, that would be the first place anybody would look. Low as the river was, they'd surely find him too.

I took out my tin and papers and rolled a cigarette for to calm me more. A checkerbacker flew up from the river and lit in the white oak, its beak tapping like a hammer as it grubbed a branch. The cicadas soon started again. I looked up but the white oak leaves was so thick I couldn't see a one of them. It was like the tree itself was singing. Think hard, I told myself, remember everything you ever knew. Don't get stirred up. Stay calm and you'll figure a way. And that's what I did, flushing thoughts out in my mind like you'd flush doves from a September corn field. All the while that checkerbacker and the cicadas made their racket above me I figured what I would do, or at least try to do. I thought out the how's for a while and walked into the house.

Amy sat in the ladder-back chair, her hand laid on her stomach. Maybe she was trying to soothe the baby, maybe just herself.

"If anybody comes and asks about Holland, you say you ain't seen him," I said. "I'm going to go do what's got to be done."

"You going to bury him?"

"It's better you not know," I said. "All you need to say is what I just told you, that you ain't seen Holland Winchester today. Understand?"

Amy looked up at me and nodded, her blue eyes sorrowful.

"I didn't never think a thing this bad could happen," Amy said.

"You're near twenty years old," I said. "You've lived long enough to know once trouble comes it don't wander off on its own."

Amy teared up, not much but enough to have to dab her eyes.

"You can't cry," I said. "We're going to act like this never happened. Never a word to no one about it, not even to each other, so if you got anything to say, say it now."

"Could we just tell the truth?" Amy asked. "Tell that he wasn't going to leave us be?"

"The truth is I shot a unarmed man, a war hero," I said. "That's the only truth a jury would care about."

"I could say I did it," Amy said. "I could say he raped me."

"And then he let you press a shotgun against his chest and pull the trigger," I said, my voice tough as barbed wire. "The biggest chucklehead in this county wouldn't believe that. All that would do is get us both sent to the jailhouse, maybe get me a sit-down in the electric chair."

My back was to the window. I turned and searched till I caught sight of Sam out by the barn chewing what little grass the dog days hadn't killed.

"There's but one way," I said. "And that's to put him where nobody can ever find him. The law needs a body to claim a murder."

I turned from the window.

"I got to get to it."

The late morning light beveled through the panes and brightened Amy's face, made her yellow hair and blue eyes shine. She looked down to shirk the glare.

"We never speak again about any of this without it's to get our story straight to tell the law," I said. "Not about you and him, not any of what happened today."

Amy didn't look up.

"Yes," she said.

I went out to the shed. The first thing I did was tie three lengths of rope together with square knots. Then I got me a roll of barbed wire and a hoe. I took the collar and trace chains off Sam and led him into the shade of the white oak. I walked around Holland's body and leaned over. I swatted at the bluebottle flies and yellow jackets and then reached under Holland's arms and heisted him up.

He was heavy, heavy enough that I pondered I might have to call Amy to help me. The stubble on Holland's face prickled my cheek while I hugged him against my chest. A yellow jacket stung me on the neck and I felt the poison riffle through my skin like scalding water.

Then I steadied Sam and grabbed Holland at his middle and shoved him onto Sam's back. I looped the rope around Holland's neck and ankles and tied him to Sam like a saddle. There was a lot more rope than I needed, at least right then, so I wrapped it around Sam a few times and knotted it under his belly.

I picked up the hoe and shotgun and laid the roll of barbed wire across my shoulder like a haversack. The barbs jabbed my shoulder like thorns on a devil's walking stick. There was nothing to be done about that. The ground stained dark where Holland had laid but the dust had already drank up his blood. Another few minutes and you wouldn't be able to tell a man's life had spilled out there. Amy came out on the porch but she didn't say anything. We was past words now.

I led Sam down the field edge past corn stalks and beans near dead as Holland. For better or worse, I thought as I rubbed my neck and almost laughed because it was hard to reckon knowing worse than this. But I knew that wasn't certain so. Things can always get worse. If what I had in mind didn't work they'd soon get a whole lot worse.

I left the hoe on the cabbage row closest to the river. I led Sam a few yards downstream to a pool that held a big brown trout I'd been trying to catch for two years. I'd used everything from hellgrammites to spring lizards and hadn't got much as a nibble. I couldn't outsmart a fish with a brain the size of a butter bean but here I was trying to outslick a sheriff who'd passed most of his life catching people like me.

I shucked off my shoes and left them on the bank. Then I wrapped the rein around my hand between my thumb and fingers and made a fist. I grabbed up the shotgun and stepped into the shallows at the tail end of the pool. Sam followed me off the bank, the water raising to my kneecaps. The water ran slow, the stones under our feet green and slick. I took my time, tucking my feet in white pockets of sand amongst the rocks. Sam stepped his way careful too, careful but calm, not shying the way many a horse would when the water got deeper. I watched Sam take another step away from a field he'd never work again. It made me sick to the heart knowing what I was going to do to him.

I tried to think of other things, letting my mind jump around in all directions like grasshoppers flaring out of high weeds. My mind lit down on nothing good, just thought-pictures of my daddy laid out dead in his coffin, Holland and Amy tangled together, me in bed as a boy with my legs froze up with polio. Don't think, Billy, I said to myself, just do.

Halfway across Sam's legs splayed out in front of him. He near went tumbling and kicking into the whitewater downstream, taking me and Holland with him, but he found his balance. We got the rest of the way without slipping and sloshed out of the river onto Carolina Power land. The power company didn't allow hunting or logging so there wouldn't be many folks poking around these woods. I thought that might be important in the later on.

I'd turned to help Sam up the bank when I saw her. She was so far upriver you could just make out it was a woman, a woman coming my way. It had to be Sarah Winchester, looking for her boy. That thought paled me. I tethered Sam in the trees deep enough not to be spotted. I carried the shotgun with me as I walked back to the river.

She was closer now, an old woman dressed in black, some kind of tote-sack in her hand. It wasn't Sarah Winchester though. It was Widow Glendower. She stopped every so often, stooping that creaky old body of hers to pick something off the riverbank. I'd watched her in past times do much the same, mainly in the spring, passing by without never a word or nod as I'd worked in my field.

I'd as lief it be the same now but I couldn't chance that. I walked upriver, not exact sure what to say or do, wondering if maybe she saw me before I saw her. A woman that old won't have good eyesight, I told myself. Don't fret yourself more than you need to.

"I take it you're Billy," she said when I stepped close. "Your woman told me ever much about you when she came calling."

She gave me a little smile I didn't much cotton to.

"Amy ain't been to see me lately. She ain't feeling poorly, is she? Ain't got the morning throw-ups?"

Widow Glendower nodded at the tote-sack she'd laid on the ground.

"I got some mint in there if she's needful. Got some boneset too."

"She's doing fine," I said.

"What of you? You look to be some peaked."

"I got no complainings."

"You certain of that?" Widow Glendower asked. "I don't mind the sharing."

"I've no need for your tonics."

Maybe it was all of what I'd been through this morning or maybe just rememberings of following that old woman's notions last spring but my words came out quarrelsome. But there was something else. I was sudden afraid of her.

Widow Glendower picked up her tote-sack.

"Well, I'll be on my way," she said. "I need to find me some yellowroot."

I stepped in front of her.

"You best not go downriver," I said.

"And why might that be?"

"There's a big satinback, twelve rattles on him at the least. I saw him sunning on a rock yesterday."

"That why you got your shotgun with you? For to kill snakes?"

I nodded.

"Well, I best stay clear of a satinback that big, for sure when the Dog Star's out. You tell that pretty wife of yours to come see me when she can make the time."

I nodded but I'd no more tell Amy such a thing than I'd tell Widow Glendower I'd killed Holland. Little enough good had already come from Amy's passing time with that old woman.

She started up the trail. I knew I needed to get a move on but I wasn't doing a thing till that old woman was a good ways upriver.

Widow Glendower had gone a good quarter-furlong when she turned around.

"I hope you killed him," she said.

Or at least that's what I reckoned I heard. I just stared at her, my right hand gripping that shotgun tight. Then I took a couple of steps toward her.

"What was your words?" I said. My voice had no more strength to it than a shadow. My body either. The shotgun felt to be a plow-point weighting my hand.

"That snake," Widow Glendower said. "I hope you kill him."

She turned and walked on, the tote-sack swaying in her hand. I didn't move till she was out of sight. Then I stepped lively to do what had to be done.

I led Sam downriver, looking for a white oak off in the woods a ways from the water, a big one but with a limb low enough for to reach. We walked the length of a tobacco row before I found what I needed in a stand of yellow poplar. I led Sam through some briars and scrub oaks thick and tangly as a laurel hell. Then the woods opened up some. I passed through the stand of yellow poplar and there stood the white oak, a good sixty foot tall but with a limb I could grip onto and then another I could gain above it.

I laid down the shotgun and the barbed wire. I tied Sam to a poplar sapling and took the rope off and leaned Holland's back against the white oak's trunk, his legs sprawled out in front of him. His eyes was still open and that grievened me enough to lean down and close them. I'd heard tell you could see the face of the killer froze in a dead man's eyes. I didn't want to know the which nor whether of that.

I looped the rope around my free shoulder and grabbed a holding on the lowliest limb and pulled myself up. I gained back my breath and reached for the next limb and heisted myself limb by limb to where the tree turkey-tailed and three limbs thick as my leg reached out in different directions.

I straddled the biggest limb and threw the knotted rope end across the branch above it. I eased the rope down through the limbs till the knot end touched the ground. I looked upriver. It took a few seconds but I finally found Widow Glendower, already up near where Wolf Creek came in. She was making a stout pace for such a old woman and I was ever so glad for that. The farther away she was the more eased my mind.

I looked far downriver and saw a Carolina Power truck parked at the end of a skid trail. Two men stood beside the truck. They was dressed in town clothes so I didn't much figure them to come through the woods my way. But I still kept my eyes on them.

"Carolina Power's going to cork this whole valley up and make them a lake," Roy Whitmire had claimed last fall after the timber company sold out. "If you ain't got a houseboat you best find another place to live."

"They can't never run us out if we don't sell," Travis Alexander had said. "And there's not a price they can offer that'll buy out me and Daddy."

"Carolina Power owns every politician in South Carolina," Roy had said. "They'll do what they damn well please. Just ask them farmers that lived down there where Santee-Cooper Reservoir is."

The two Carolina Power men soon got in the truck and drove

toward Tamassee. I reckoned Roy was right about a lake coming but that had all seemed so in the far-off I hadn't fretted much on it. There wasn't no need to now either. I had troubles enough in the here and now.

I shimmied on down and tied one rope end under Holland's arms and the other around Sam's neck. I pushed and twisted the roll of barbed wire over Holland's head till it laid around his neck like a yoke. The barbs tore into his face and back of his head in the most awful kind of way but I knew in my heart it was not near as awful as taking his life.

I took Sam's rein and walked with him out into the stand of yellow poplar, Holland's body circling slow as it raised into the sky like a body caught in a suckhole below a waterfall. I looked at Holland dangling from that white oak and tried not to see it as a sign of my own future.

The rope spread Holland's arms out. They was stiff now as fire-pokers and as he raised higher his arms looked like wings. I remembered Preacher Robertson reading from Revelation how on Judgment Day the dead would raise from earth and sea and fly to heaven and what a glorious sight that would be. But as I patted Sam's flank and Holland lifted another few yards toward the sky, his face gouged by barbed wire, the hole in his chest boiling with bluebottle flies and yellow jackets, I reckoned a man might witness no more terrible sight than the dead resurrected.

When Holland reached the big limb I stopped Sam and told him to stay. I climbed back in the tree and geed and hawed till Holland's body laid near the lengthwise of the limb. I gripped onto the rope with one hand as I straddled Holland's chest and wrapped my legs around him and the limb like a bear hug.

It was a tricky business. I got stung twice more by yellow jackets and without Sam holding steady I'd of never got it done. I uncoiled the barbed wire with my free hand, letting it dangle down till it almost stretched to the ground.

When only two strands was left on Holland's neck I tightened and twisted them together and then started wrapping the rest of the barbed wire around him, starting with his shoulders and then over his arms and then every few inches till it was down to his ankles. I wrapped it tight and close as bark on a tree, mashing the arms against his sides, letting the barbs cut deep in his skin.

It seemed like it took forever and I had to stop several times to rest and dab some tobacco on my stings. I was high enough to see Mrs. Winchester's house as well as mine. Smoke curled from the chimney and I reckoned Mrs. Winchester was cooking noon-dinner and there was probably a place set at the table that would never be filled again.

That fire was a good sign for me. She wasn't worried enough yet to trouble the sheriff. As I worked I wondered if Holland had pondered much about the men he'd killed. I wondered if he'd dreamed about them or said prayers for them. I said a prayer right then for Holland and asked him and God to forgive me—not just for the killing but what I was doing now, for many of the older folks argued a soul couldn't rest easy till it was in godly earth.

But it was a sorry excuse for a prayer, asking nothing more of me than some muttered words and I figured it had about as much chance being heard in heaven as a hog's fart.

When I finally finished I didn't climb down. I needed to think out what questions Sheriff Alexander might offer up and how I would answer. He was a smart man, like every Alexander I ever knew, and he'd had some college down at Clemson. I sat and tried to think through all and every question and how I'd answer.

"No, I ain't seen Holland Winchester," I said right out loud, trying to calm each word as it left my lips.

I tarried in the white oak a while longer. Being that high up it was like I could have a good look around not just at the countryside but at my life. I'd broke quite a sweat getting Holland tied to that limb and the hard work had settled my mind the way hard work sometimes can. I thought about me and Amy and our getting to the other side of all that had happened. For we would, though I wasn't certain sure of the how yet.

In a few minutes Mrs. Winchester came outside. She opened Holland's truck door and mashed the horn a couple of times before walking into the woods that bordered our farms. She laid her hands on the fence and called Holland's name. Then she walked back out of the trees and headed for the fields and woods on the other side of her house. I could see her raise her hands to her mouth though I couldn't hear her.

I climbed down and raveled the rope off Sam, then climbed back up the tree and tied the rope around Holland as well. I had him wrapped tight as sewing thread on a spool. I reckoned even a tornado couldn't shake him free of that limb.

When I got back down I took up the shotgun and used the barrel to nuzzle Sam behind the ears where he'd always liked to be scratched. He'd been as good a plow horse as I'd ever been around, even-tempered and strong and ever reliable as the sun rising. He stepped nimble as any mule between the crop rows and unlike many another plow horse he never startled when the plow hit a stump or rock. I'd been with Sam longer than I'd been with Amy. Even after me and her got married I spent more waking hours in the springs and summers with him than I had her. I'd talked to him the way you can't help but talk to any animal you've been around a lot.

"That corn's not going to make it, Sam," I'd say, or "We'll have rain by afternoon, Sam."

I believed he'd had a reckoning of what I was saying, even if it wasn't word for word, the way a person would understand. That reckoning was me and him working together hard as we could to make a living from this scratch-ankle mountain land but no matter how hard we worked there'd be things me and him couldn't do nothing about. All we could do was keep the reins tight and hope for the best.

Sam snorted. He knew it was near noon-dinner time. He was ready to get across the river and graze by the barn while I ate my cornbread and beans.

"You been a good plow horse, Sam," I said, "and I wouldn't do this if there was any other way."

Then I settled the barrel deeper in the soft spot behind his ear and mashed the trigger.

I made sure he was dead before I broke his leg with a rock.

~

When I came up the bank I saw the groundhog at the far end of the row. I didn't bother to load the chamber and take a shot at him. I didn't feel like killing nothing else.

The sun read past noon but I figured it best to be in my field if the law showed up. Besides, I had no appetite. I picked up the hoe and walked to where me and Sam had stopped that morning. I knew it was going to be a lot slower and burdensome the rest of the summer working with only my two hands to get things done. I knew even if the tobacco did well I'd be buying a mule or plow horse come fall with a good part of that money.

I started chopping at the weeds like I was chopping at a copperhead or satinback, because bad thoughts was loose in my head again. I was hoping if I worked hard enough I could push them out of my mind. Every time I hit a rock sparks flew and the handle jarred my hand like a jolt of electricity. Sweat riffled off my face and though my palms was calloused I gripped the hoe so hard I raised a couple of blisters. I didn't look up. The only way I knew I was at the end of the row was when the hoe hit tall grass.

But bad thoughts kept swirling in my head no matter how

fierce I banged that hoe into the ground. I started thinking what if Amy turncoated me the second the law arrived and told everything of what had happened? Or maybe she'd planned for me to kill Holland all along, that she'd never loved me, just used me to get gone from her parents' house and having to help look after eight shirt-tail brothers and sisters. I pondered what if Holland was somehow still alive up in that white oak calling for help. Or Widow Glendower had said what I first reckoned her to have said. Or Holland's momma had heard the shot that morning and called the law right away and the law had been watching while I took Holland's body and hid it in the white oak—that the law was in the woods right now watching, getting ready to step out from behind a tree and arrest me.

I raised up and looked toward the woods. I gripped the hoe across my chest, the blade end up, ready to swing at anybody who stepped near. But there wasn't nobody coming out of the woods or up at the house talking to Amy. The only sound coming from the trees across the river was cicadas. Keep your head, I told myself. I took deep, slow breaths till my mind cleared like it does when a fever breaks. I started hoeing again, but slower. Slow and steady, I told myself. You got a long ways to go.

~

Sheriff Alexander showed up late in the afternoon. I was finishing a row when I heard my name. I turned and there he was, wearing his big black hat that made him look more preacher than law man. He acted all casual, as like he was just out for his constitutional and happened to have ended up in my tobacco field.

"How you doing, Sheriff."

I said it calm as a cat's purr and looking straight into his gray eyes.

"I'm looking for Holland Winchester," he said. "You seen

him?"

"No," I said, keeping my eyes fixed on his.

He let that stand without a word edgewise.

"Well if you see him, tell him he's got his momma worried."

"I'll do that, Sheriff," I said. He didn't say no word more, just turned and limped out of the field but I could tell he had his suspectings about me. I knew I'd be seeing him again and that next time he wouldn't be so easy satisfied. I knew me and him was just getting started.

I hoed another hour and then went to the house. Amy didn't say a word but she hugged me. I hadn't reckoned how much I'd needed that hug till right then. We held each other a long time, long enough that I checked out the window to make sure Sheriff Alexander hadn't felt need to wander my land some more.

I told Amy what she needed to know. Then we set down at the table.

I made myself eat all of what filled my plate. I knew I'd need all the strength I could gain up the next day or two but the field peas and potatoes had no flavor. The cornbread stuck in my throat like sand. Amy pushed her portion around the plate with her fork. She managed a few bites only after I reminded her she was eating for the young one too.

Amy looked bone tired and for the first time I glimsened how she'd look when she wasn't young and pretty anymore. I knew that wouldn't be far along, because life on a hill farm wears down a woman faster than a man, at least on the outside. Momma once told how she'd stared in the looking glass one day and not realized herself for a second. "Who is that old woman staring at me," she'd thought.

She'd been all of thirty years old.

"I'll start on a baby crib tomorrow evening," I said, because I'd as lief give Amy a happy thought on a day when me or her hadn't had many.

I gave her a smile or at least as close to a smile as I could counterfeit.

"Go lay down for a while," I said. "You and that baby need some rest."

"I think I will," Amy said and went on to the back room.

I stepped out on the porch. I wanted to study some more about what I was going to say if Sheriff Alexander showed back up before dark with some questions. But he didn't show and after a while the sun fell behind Sassafras Mountain and shadows stretched out till they wasn't shadows anymore. The lightning bugs moved low across the yard like little lanterns. Cicadas sang in the trees and down by the river bullfrogs jabbered at one another on the banks. I got up from the steps and went inside. I undressed quiet as I could and eased into bed.

Amy's back was to me but when I nudged up close and laid my hand on her belly, she turned. Her hand touched the back of my head and led my lips to hers as she laid her flesh against mine. We hadn't in several months, not since I'd got my suspicions about her and Holland Winchester. Amy's bosoms felt fuller now, like they was already filled with baby milk, and her belly was curved and firm.

For a little while it was like I was drifting away from everything that had happened since Holland came into the yard that morning. Each thought-picture of Holland dying or dead that seemed nailed inside my head got smaller and smaller till it was near no longer there. It must have been the same for Amy. Her breath was deep and fast as mine. We cleaved together like we was drowning and could only be saved by each other.

I slept a few hours, a sleep so black and deep beyond even dreams. I woke in the dark. For a moment I laid there not even recollecting what had happened yesterday. Then it all came rushing on me like a dam broke open and I knew no matter how long I laid there I'd not gain a wink of sleep more. Amy didn't stir as I slipped on my overalls and brogans.

I walked out to the well and drew water to splash the sleep off my face, then took a step toward the barn out of habit but there was nothing waiting in there for me now. I sat on the porch steps and went over again what I'd say when the law showed back up. Sheriff Alexander would want to talk and there'd be a sight more to it than "Have you seen Holland Winchester?"

After a while first light came drizzling through the trees. I spotted the Dog Star between the white oak's branches. To its right was another star my daddy always made claim was the planet Venus.

I got up when I heard Amy making breakfast, my back stiff from all I did the day before. I forked my biscuit and gravy down quick, then stepped out on the porch.

"Do you have to go so soon?" Amy asked.

"I want the sheriff to find me in my field," I said, "out in the open like a man with nothing to hide."

Amy reached her hand and touched my arm, like after all of what had happened she needed to be sure I was flesh and blood, like she reckoned all of this a dream.

I picked up the hoe and the .12 gauge.

"If this ain't nothing but a dream I'm in it with you," I said.

The high grass at the field edge darkened my brogans with dew. The sun hadn't livelied up the grasshoppers so they just hung on the stalks when I brushed past. Wisps of fog curled off the river. I laid down the shotgun and got to my work.

As I hoed cabbage my mind was on last night, how good it had felt to be one flesh again with Amy, how it had been a kind of first step back to the way things had once been between us. I recollected how it had been that December morning when Doctor Griffen had showed up for his weekly visit. He poked my legs like always but this time my leg muscles quivered, as like he'd jolted electricity into them.

"I think he's going to be all right," Doctor Griffen said. "It'll be a slow healing but he'll get there."

"Thank you, God," Momma said, falling to her knees and praying out loud in front of Doctor Griffen and me and Daddy.

But it took a while. Daddy had to build me crutches to perch my arms on. It was a slow going at first but after a couple days I'd got to hobbling around the house pretty good. Doctor Griffen had checked me again a week later.

"You don't need those crutches anymore," he'd said.

But I did, because I doubted my legs after so long a time. It had been another week before I took my first steps, holding onto the porch railing when I did, then finally letting go. That was how it was with Amy after months of doubting her. I had learned to trust Doctor Griffen and my legs. Now I had to gain up trust in Amy and my own heart.

~

I saw the first buzzard when I finished my third row, so high up it was no bigger seeming than a gnat.

The next time I looked there was four. They came down slow, tightening their circle the way you'd tighten the lid on a mason jar. Or a noose around a neck, and that thought didn't set very well with me. You knew they'd come, I told myself. You'd counted on it. Still, seeing those buzzards sent a tremble through my bones.

I hoed the last of the cabbage, then laid the hoe and shotgun at the end of the first tobacco row. I kneeled down and rubbed a green leaf between my finger and thumb, the same way you'd rub a dollar bill, because that's what it was, money. Which was the why for giving over my best piece of land to it and the why for though the beans and corn might not make it we'd get through the winter, provided I was around to harvest and cure it. But we'd be eating a lot of cabbage come January and February and we'd be eating it by lamplight.

I started topping the tobacco, pulling off what worms I found, a good many as it turned out, every one of them big as my thumb. The sun climbed up over the trees and sweat slicked my arms and face.

It wasn't long before I heard a bloodhound giving tongue over at Mrs. Winchester's. In a couple of minutes it came out of the woods with a couple of men following. The dog went right for the white oak there in the yard, poked its nose to the very spot where Holland had laid. It circled for a couple of minutes around the white oak but you could tell the trail had gone cold. One of the men leashed the bloodhound and they walked back toward Mrs. Winchester's.

Then I saw the other men, moving out of the woods like a army, sticks in their hands like rifles. It seemed a hundred of them, moving through the yard and into the pasture and woods behind the house. Like the buzzards, it wasn't nothing I hadn't expected but it was still a bothersome sight.

I tried to put my head down and tend to my tobacco but I kept peeking toward the house. Soon enough the men who'd followed the bloodhound into the yard came back out of the woods. A fourth man was with them now and I could tell from the black preacher's hat it was Sheriff Alexander. They passed some words then split up.

Three men walked towards me. They didn't have the dog with them and their hands hauled things now. The lead man was Bobby Murphree. The man behind him I couldn't put a name on but the last one was Tom Watson, who'd gone to school with me and Holland.

Sheriff Alexander went up on the porch. Amy came to the door and they talked a minute before he stepped inside. I didn't like that for I wanted them in my sight but there was no more than nothing I could do about it.

Bobby Murphree and the other man only nodded when they passed. They was shutmouth and serious. It was obvious they had suspicions against me. But Tom Watson lagged behind them a ways.

"I'll not hold it against you if you did kill the son of a bitch," Tom said out the corner of his mouth. "I'd of been likely to do it my own self given half a chance."

I didn't say a word to that. I just kept on topping the tobacco plants, not looking in their direction till they'd disappeared down the riverbank. The sun looked midmorning but I was already tired and thirsty. I didn't want to leave my field though for that might look queer. I kept on moving down the rows, pulling off leaves and worms and keeping my head down best as I could.

The ground trembled under my feet when the first stick of dynamite went off. It was loud enough to raise the dead but the dead was already raised up in that white oak. There was another big boom a few minutes later. You could easy enough follow them as they worked their way downriver. It seemed they didn't walk no more than a few feet before they lit another stick of dynamite. They seemed likely to blast every puddle the dog days had left in that river.

Then I saw Sheriff Alexander. He was wearing his uniform today, letting me and everybody else know he hadn't come up here to trifle. Momma had once recollected us and the Alexanders was kin on her side. I wondered if he recognized us as relations.

I stood tall and watched him come as another dynamite stick boomed downriver. He knew well as me that I'd spotted him. There was no use of counterfeiting I hadn't.

Sheriff Alexander stepped past where my hoe and .12 gauge laid. I knew right then Amy had said never a word he could get me on. He stood at the end of the row I'd been working, not looking at me but across the river. He looked like he was twice reading something to make sure it said what he thought it said.

He finally looked my way.

"Looks to be something dead over yonder."

I never gave it a glance.

"It's my plow horse. He broke his leg yesterday."

I said it pretty as a potato bug and I didn't stumble a word. He didn't reckon me to say anything like that. I could tell by the way he rechecked the sky it set him back, that the message he'd read up there wasn't near as clear as it had been a few seconds before.

"That's some hard luck," Sheriff Alexander finally said.

"Yes sir," I said. "It is."

"Is it in the river?"

"No, back in the woods a ways."

"We'll go over and have us a look-see directly."

He looked at the tobacco plants, his glasses slipping a little down his nose.

"You'll make some good money this fall," he said.

"I reckon."

"So you didn't see Holland yesterday?" he asked, changing the subject slick as a peeled onion.

"No," I said.

"Your wife said she hadn't either, but I got cause to wonder about that."

Sheriff Alexander pursed his lips to say something else but didn't get a chance. The other men came stumbling up the bank toward us. Bobby Murphree was in the lead, Tom Watson and the other man following him.

"Bring up anything?" Sheriff Alexander asked.

Tom Watson opened his canvas pack.

"Nothing but this," he said, lifting up the big brown I'd tried to catch for two years. He reached it out to Sheriff Alexander, his finger hooked in the gills.

"Twenty-three inches long," Tom Watson said, joggling it on his fingers. "Five pounds if it's a ounce."

"Did you see what was drawing them buzzards?" Sheriff Alexander asked, nodding at the tree line.

The men turned toward the river.

"Damn," Bobby Murphree said. "I guess we was looking down when we should of been looking up."

Bobby Murphree didn't know the truth of that but I wasn't about to help him notion it. In a couple of minutes him and Tom and the other man left, taking my .12 gauge with them. It was just me and Sheriff Alexander again, the way I reckoned he wanted it.

Sheriff Alexander bent his knees and squatted. I could hear his knees pop and he gave a grunt as he put out his hand to balance himself. He was letting me know he'd be visiting a while. He took his nose rag from his back pocket and cleaned his glasses. He wiped his face though there wasn't more than a drop or two of sweat on him, just expecting there to be because he'd lived down in Seneca too long. He was used to a place where the air got thick like water and sweat lathered your skin if you did anything more than sit and fan yourself. He'd forgot that up here you had to be working to break a full sweat, even in the dog days.

Sheriff Alexander didn't put his glasses back on right then. He just looked up and let his gray eyes fix on me like a hawk's eyes on a meadow mouse.

"I'm going to lay it all out on the table for you, Billy," he said. "Then I'll let you have your say."

Sheriff Alexander put his glasses back on. They made his eyes bigger, not so much anymore like hawk's eyes as owl's eyes.

He went at me pretty lively for a few minutes, trying to rile me, get me to say something I'd not meant to. But I didn't rise to his bait.

"Let's go have a look at that horse," he finally said.

We waded the same shallows where I'd crossed Sam, then walked down the river and into the woods. If you can get through this you'll be O.K., I said in my mind. I kept telling myself that till we stepped into the stand of yellow poplar.

Buzzards covered Sam like a quilt. You couldn't see a bit of hide and there was a dozen other buzzards skipping and flapping around looking for openings to poke their beaks in. More was up in the trees. I could hear them flapping and rustling up there but how many I couldn't say. I kept my eyes looking down.

Sheriff Alexander put the nose rag to his face and waded in amongst the buzzards, kicking at them till they scattered enough to give him a gander. Then he stepped back and the buzzards closed back in on Sam like knottyheads on stickbait.

"Let's get the hell out of here," he said, and I didn't argue otherwise.

We crossed the river and I stepped back into the field to finish topping the tobacco.

Sheriff Alexander watched me a couple of minutes. I wondered if he recollected what it was like not to have a steady paycheck, to work months and not know if you'd make money that year or not. I wondered if he recollected how it's a different sun in August, a sun that lays heavier on a man's shoulders, like maybe the Dog Star's mashing its weight down on you as well. Maybe he did remember. Maybe that was why he lived and worked in town.

"I got to go back to Seneca for a while," he finally said. "But I got one question I've been puzzling over. How'd you get a horse with a broke leg across that river?"

That was a question I hadn't figured to be asked. Sheriff Alexander's eyes watched me and didn't blink. Owl eyes, I thought, wise eyes that don't miss a thing. I had to think out a answer and put a bridle on my tongue till I was sure I had it. Cicadas sang in the trees, making it harder to crosshair my mind. I finally rooted up a likely-seeming answer.

I could tell what I spoke didn't satisfy him but he just walked on up the field edge to his car. Sheriff Alexander drove back to Seneca and I went to the house for noon-dinner.

~

They came back in the afternoon. Five cars of searchers flocked in my yard, Sheriff Alexander giving them their orders. Then it was like a army again, this time wading across the river and moving up the east slope of Licklog Mountain. Sheriff Alexander and Bobby Murphree searched at the house while Tommy Watson and another man was grappling in the river some more. I stayed in my field, topping and worming my tobacco, trying my best not to act like I knew there was thirty men searching every inch of my farm to get me in the electric chair.

I quit my work before they did, walking back to the house for my supper. The gloaming set in before they gave up. The searchers came straggling back out of the shadow of Licklog Mountain. All they had to show for their work was chigger bites and beggar lice. They piled back in their cars and Sheriff Alexander and Bobby Murphree got in their car too. Amy was putting up the supper dishes but I lagged by the window as Sheriff Alexander's law car bumped down the washout. As I watched I figured me and Amy had got through the tangliest part of the briar patch. If we could hold on to our story a couple more days we'd be O.K.

Then I saw the brake lights come on, glowing red in the gloaming like blood. Sheriff Alexander turned the car around.

"He's coming back," I told Amy.

In that second I felt feather-legged as the moment I'd shot Holland. I knew he'd thought of something, something that wouldn't wait for a tomorrow. He came up on the porch and knocked on the door jamb. He knocked confident.

"Come on," he said, and nodded me toward the car where Bobby Murphree poked around in the trunk, "and bring a lantern. We need to go back over to where that horse is."

When he said that I felt my heart start beating against my ribs like a quail caught in a snare. Calm down, I said to myself. I glanced at Amy and saw there was some scared in her too. For a second I thought of going for the ax next to the kindling. But it was just that, a thought. I'd killed one more man than enough for me.

Amy reached me a lantern and I lit it.

"Step ahead of us and be the bell-cow," Sheriff Alexander said. "I'd rather see a snake before I put my foot down on him."

"What you got on your mind, Sheriff?" Bobby Murphree asked as we followed the field edge to the water.

"Maybe just a snipe hunt, but I don't think so."

The strut in his words laid heavy on my mind as we waded across. I recollected what I'd heard about the Columbia jailhouse, the way men lived in packs like wolves and did things you wouldn't want to dwell on to those that wasn't a part of their pack. I was thinking I'd be looking forward to the state killing me after a few months being sport for such men.

But I knew that to be a lie quick as I thought it. I'd still want to live, no matter what men might do to me in jail. If I did have to die I couldn't think of no worse way than a sit-down in the electric chair.

I led Sheriff Alexander and Bobby Murphree into the woods, walking slow, waving the lantern low in front of me for Sheriff Alexander was right that copperheads and satinbacks liked to crawl at night. My mind was near as fevered as it had been when I killed Holland, for I recollected what I'd been told about Ansel Crowe when the state killed him for a murder over in Long Creek.

His family went down to Columbia for the execution. Ansel's brother had told me how they'd watched through a big piece of glass while the guards strapped Ansel in and then put a hood over his face. That had made it worse, because Ansel was jerking his head all every way to keep them from getting the hood on, trying to gain himself a few seconds. When they'd turned on the electricity Ansel's body had tried to raise up out of the chair. His hood had caught fire like a struck match. The warden had told Ansel's family he'd felt never a thing but like Ansel's brother had said, how the hell did that warden know what Ansel had felt.

I tried not to think about Ansel but I couldn't forget it. The lantern got trembly in my hand. Only the dark kept Sheriff Alexander from knowing the state I was in.

You'll walk this slow when they take you to the electric chair, I said in my mind but it was as like the woods had whispered it to me. My legs buckled and I almost fell. If I had I'd of been too feather-legged to get up. I'd of probably broke down and confessioned it all right then and there.

"Watch yourself," Sheriff Alexander said.

Yes, I told myself, watch yourself. Don't give yourself away. Make them show Holland's body to you. I took slow breaths trying to settle myself as we stopped in front of the white oak.

A possum wiggled out of a hole in Sam's flank like it was getting born. It was bloated like a tick, its belly rubbing the ground. The possum raised its bat face and hissed before heading toward the river.

"We got to move that horse," Sheriff Alexander said.

He looked at Bobby Murphree.

"Do you think if we put a rope around its neck we could drag it a few yards?"

I didn't know the exact of what he was studying. What I did know was he hadn't raised that lantern toward the white oak's branches or told Bobby Murphree to shimmy up the tree. Keep calm, I told myself for the hundredth time since dawn, and keep a bridle on your mouth.

"We can try," Bobby Murphree said.

He made a noose and tightened it around Sam's neck. He didn't take a breath while he did it and came back over to us sucking air like he'd been underwater.

"You help too," Sheriff Alexander said to me.

The three of us gripped the rope end and dragged Sam till Sheriff Alexander said stop. He took the shovel and stepped to where Sam had laid and stabbed the ground a few times.

Sheriff Alexander looked up at me like I had doublecrossed him somehow and I knew if he didn't reckon where Holland was in the next minute or so he never would if he lived a hundred years. Because he was shutting away a possibility the same way you nail a board over a well you're sure has gone dry.

We recrossed the river. As we came up the bank I smelled rain. The cicadas had quieted some and I reckoned they smelled it too. I wondered if maybe there was something to killing blacksnakes after all.

"I'll see you tomorrow," Sheriff Alexander said when we got to the house. "Who knows what might turn up, especially after a good rain."

But his voice had no swagger like it had earlier. He was fishing with a bare hook and the both of us knew it.

I stepped inside the house and watched the law car's red tail lights disappear down the washout. This time Sheriff Alexander didn't stop and turn around.

"I think everything is going to be all right," I told Amy, and she nodded. She came over and hugged me, the baby pressing my belly.

"There have been times of late I'd never have believed it," Amy said. "But I almost can now."

I kissed Amy on the cheek.

"I'm out to the shed to start on that crib."

"You ain't obliged to just for me," Amy said. "It can wait if you're wore out."

"I don't mind none," I said. "I won't tarry longer than to get a start on it."

I poked around the shed a while and finally settled on some wild cherry I'd put an axe to last winter. It was pretty wood and I knew it would please Amy. I sat down at my lathe and busied myself, pumping the lathe and working the wood with the chisel. The lantern light was shadowy but it was enough. The wild cherry had a bright smell, like honeysuckle. The breeze made the shed door creak.

Bring that rain this way, wind, I said to myself, bring enough to keep me out of my fields and in this shed come tomorrow, a big enough rain to wash the Dog Star out of the sky. That wood felt right and comfortable in my hands. It was a happy kind of work making that crib and I soon lost myself in it, the way you can when you're doing something pleasing.

Amy came to fetch me after a while, though it was hard to know if ten minutes or two hours had passed. We went to bed and joined flesh again. It was different than the night before, not so much needful but sweet and contenting.

Afterward I laid there, my hand on Amy's belly. For the first time I duly felt that young one was mine too and that damped my eyes. I made promises to myself and to God to be a good daddy. I thought about the sinner on the cross Jesus had saved and prayed God and Jesus to forgive me. Unlike my prayer in the white oak, I reckoned this one might have a chance of being heard.

I felt the baby kick and at the same moment the window lighted up. Signs of new beginnings, I thought. The cicadas was hushed in the trees and it was like the whole world was quiet and listening. A breeze lifted the curtains on the window. I heard the first grumble of thunder coming across Sassafras Mountain.

It wasn't long before drops of rain tapped the roof and that's the best sound ever I've known to make a body drowsy. I knew if I rathered I could be asleep quick as a cat. But I didn't want to sleep yet, because for the first time in months I didn't feel a loneliness in my heart. I just wanted to lay there with that good feeling awhile.

Amy nuzzled her back closer to my chest. The rain came harder, settling in like a dog settles in front of a hearth. I let my thoughts carry out the window to the corn and beans and the splats of rain turning dust back to dirt. I thought of the roots sipping up that rain and it raising through stalks and stems like a river reversing and going up its prongs. I knew many of my plants it was too late for but some would make it. That was a high yield to what I'd of expected yesterday.

I felt the young one stir again and told myself my luck had changed, was changing with every drop of rain that fell on my thirsty fields. Next spring I'd plant just tobacco in my bottomlands and I'd have electricity and a new truck come harvest time. That's what I told myself as I let sleep fall over me like warm rain.

~

It was the first week in November when I went back across the river, on a scawmy morning when fog covered the fields like the earth itself was smoldering. I carried a shovel and burlap cabbage sack. Out hunting sang, I'd say, if I happened on anyone, though that was ever so doubtful on such a dismal morning.

Sam was nothing but bones and patches of hair moldering into the ground. I shoveled out a hole to bury what was left of him and the ground was boggy enough to make it easy work. I wanted to believe there was something more of him somewhere. I knew the Bible claimed no soul for a animal but I wanted to believe part of Sam somehow lived on. If it wasn't a soul like a man's maybe it was some kind of happy lingering of what it had felt to rest easy in the barn after a hard day dragging a plow.

Then I climbed the white oak. Holland had a tuft of hair on his head but the rest of him was nothing more than bones held together by barbed wire and rope. I loosed the wire and rope and let him fall. A foot and arm broke free and the head scattered off under a poplar sapling.

After I shimmied down I used the shovel to snap Holland's backbone in two. I broke off his legs and the other arm and poked out the cabbage sack with his bones. I picked up the head last. That's when I saw the dog tags laying on the ground. Seeing the dog tags was a bothersome thing, though I couldn't say the exact why of that.

I walked a good quarter mile deeper into the woods, moving up the east face of Licklog. I found a big white ash and let that be the spot. Since the ground wasn't froze, getting Holland buried was no hard chore. I dug a hole a good three feet and laid the sack in the bottom. I shoveled the dirt back in, then scuttled leaves over where I'd dug and stepped off a ways. You couldn't tell the ground had ever been bothered.

"You got away with it," Sheriff Alexander had said that last afternoon he came, and in some ways it had all been unsettling easy. A part of me troubled over that, because I knew there was a price to be paid some way or another. Even if the state of South Carolina didn't collect that price, sooner or later God would. That thief on the cross was forgiven but he still had to hang there and hurt. I recollected how Mark warned about the sins of the father being laid on the child. The closer to the baby coming, the more that verse troubled my mind.

Maybe it was traipsing out in the woods on such a drizzly morning but the next day I felt out of sorts. I figured it for a cold and reckoned it would pass in a couple days. But it didn't pass. By December I could hardly raise out of bed.

When the baby came, I tried to be of some good but it drooped me to do the least little thing. But sick as I was, I was ever so eased to see the baby wasn't afflicted. They wouldn't let me hold him, which was the right thing with me ailing, but I did get to see him the day he got born. He lay there all asleep and peaceful looking, his little body scrunched up next to Amy. I studied his features careful. What sprigs of hair he had was blonde and fine as corn silk. That and the shaping of his nose and mouth made there no mistaking Amy was his momma.

By February I was no more able to raise out of bed than years back when I'd had the polio. Fever was thick upon me now. I didn't get up but to go to the outhouse and that was like walking up Whiteside Mountain. The world got all blurry and dim and I hardly knew it for day or night. All I knew certain was someone else was in that back room with me.

He leaned out of corner shadows with his dark eyes watching me with never a blink. A strand of barbed wire tore into his brow. The blood from the barbs streamed down his face like tears.

"What do you want of me?" I shouted at him, but he didn't answer.

When Amy came in to lay a fresh poultice on my brow I'd point to him in the corner. Soon as I did he melted into the shadows like black ice.

"There ain't nothing there, Billy," Amy said, but when she left he took shape in the corner again. Just standing there, waiting.

It was the tea that finally did me some good. By then I was so on the down-go I couldn't hold the cup. Amy reached it to my lips and I sipped slightly as a hummingbird.

"You got to swallow it all, Billy," Amy said, keeping that cup pressed to my lips.

Day and night for three days, every time I opened my eyes Amy had more tea for me to sip. I could feel it spreading through me, doing its work to cool my fever. Soon enough I held the cup in my hand.

The fever broke the third evening. I sat up in bed and ate something besides soup for the first time in a far while.

"You look something of your old self," Amy said, taking my

empty plate.

"I feel mostly alive," I said. "That's a come-up from where I been."

Come early morning I had to go to the outhouse. I slipped my coat over my long handles and put on my brogans. I lit the lantern and stepped outside.

A hard frost crunched under my feet. Stars speckled the sky and a wet moon snagged on the white oak's top branch. Somewhere down near the river a horned owl hooted but the rest of the night was quiet. The bullfrogs was gobbed down in river mud, the cicadas froze dead by frost.

When I'd done my business, I had a thought to check the mule I'd bought in the fall but went back to the house instead. I was still puny, like something had sapped the very marrow from my bones, but my mind and the world was clear again. I knew in a few days I'd have my strength gained up.

Amy hadn't brung the baby to the back room when she'd tended me so it had been a good month since I'd laid eyes on him. I stood by the hearth and held the lamp over the crib, looking as I always had to see Amy in his features. He slept on his back, a quilt pulled up to his shoulders, little fists no bigger than walnuts tucked under his chin like he was praying.

"Isaac," I said softly, getting used to the name. I touched his head with my fingers, what hair there was fine and yellow as corn silk. His eyelashes flickered and Holland Winchester's dark eyes stared straight into mine.

I knew then my certain future. It was like those eyes was God's hands opening palm up to show me the way it would ever be. I knew then the truth of that verse about Him seeing the fall of the sparrow. I knew He witnessed the quietest stir of a leaf, the smallest bead of water. I saw the coming years when those eyes would look at me from across the table every meal I ate, would be waiting for me every afternoon when I came from my field. I saw me and him later on working together, putting up hay, planting the fields, and all of a sudden his eyes on me and how it would feel like a icy fishhook stuck barb-deep in my heart and I'd wonder if somehow Holland was watching me from the other side.

The easy thing to do would have been to walk the four miles to the highway. Some farmer taking eggs or milk to Seneca would get me the rest of the way. If nobody was at the jailhouse I'd set down with my back against the door till Sheriff Alexander or Bobby Murphree showed up.

But I couldn't do that. No matter what Amy said that young one was Holland's too. The only way to do right by Holland was give his child shoes and a full belly and teach him how to be a man. To do those things I'd have to stay on this farm and love him for what he was—a son.

I hadn't got away with nothing.

the
SON

I WAS four years old when I first knew she was watching me. Momma had given me a puzzle to put together, so I'd laid the bright green and red pieces out on the pew while Preacher Robertson shouted about things I didn't understand. I couldn't make the puzzle pieces fit together. I'd soon given up and started fidgeting and looking all around like a kid will do in church.

I'd looked across the center aisle to the row opposite of us where Mrs. Winchester sat. Our eyes met. At that moment I realized those dark-brown eyes had watched me a long time—not just seconds or minutes but months, maybe years, and not just here in church but from across the barbed wire fence that separated her farm from ours.

Her eyes locked on mine, like there wasn't anybody else in that church but me and her. I couldn't have looked away if I'd have wanted too. Those eyes held me firm as any arms could. They were hungry eyes.

She fumbled in her pocketbook and took out a peppermint.

"After church," she said, but silently, mouthing the words.

When the last amen was said I made a beeline through the tall legs of the grown-ups to where she waited. She unwrapped the candy, and her bony fingers laid the peppermint on my tongue.

"There now, sonny," she said. "I'll bring you one of them every Sunday."

I felt Momma's hand on my shoulder, her grip firm as her voice.

"Come on, Isaac," she said, and she pulled me away from Mrs. Winchester.

"I don't want you taking candy or anything else from that old woman," Momma said in the truck. "I don't want you around her."

"Yes ma'am," I said.

But I lied.

Whenever I thought Momma and Daddy wouldn't notice, I sneaked away before or after church and found her. It was like a game of hide-and-seek, played not with other children but with grown-ups. As soon as Mrs. Winchester saw me coming she opened her ragged black pocketbook and took out a peppermint. There was hardly a word between us, like we were spies trading secrets.

After a while it wasn't just church. Sometimes when I was playing she'd show up at the fence, always when Momma was inside and Daddy in the fields.

"Here," she said, reaching through the rusty barbed wire. "You enjoy that sugar tit."

By the time I was eight I was sneaking over to her house. On days breath bloomed from my mouth in white puffs and frost or snow crunched under my feet, she poured me cups of hot chocolate. If it was hot she gave me Cheerwine or Coca-Cola in ice-cold bottles that made it taste all the better.

"How are you doing in your school-learning?" she might ask as we sat at the kitchen table, or "It looks like we'll have rain by evening."

But it always seemed she was about to say something else. She'd purse her lips as if to speak, then seem to think better of it.

It was a dark house she lived in, the shades always drawn, the lights never on. There were rifles racked on the walls. Rods and reels cluttered a corner near the door, a pair of men's boots on the floor beside them. In the kitchen a calendar yellowed above the stove, its edges curled. The month on the calendar was August, the year 1952.

Outside in the driveway was a blue pickup, at least it had once been blue. Rust had scabbed it brown but for a few flecks of paint. The tires sagged and rotted, making the truck look like it had sunk into the ground.

Such things would have been spooky to a lot of kids, especially with a snaggly-toothed old woman living alone in such a place. But I always felt cozy and comfortable there, not the least bit afraid.

Sometimes if it was cold we sat by the fire, the cup of hot chocolate cradled in my hands. On the mantle above me loomed a clock, its hands frozen at five minutes until eleven. Beside the clock was a photograph, framed and hung like a painting.

"Who is he?" I once asked.

"That's my youngest boy," she said. "You favor him, especially in the eyes."

I looked up at the man in the uniform. I studied his eyes and saw they were dark like mine, like hers.

"Where is he?"

"I don't know," she told me. "But I have a hope of someday finding out."

"So he's alive."

"No," she said. "He ain't alive."

I didn't understand that, but there are lots of things grown-ups say when you're a kid you can't figure out.

She took the cup from my hands.

"You best be getting on home. Your folks will be missing you."

That was what she always said, instead of "Don't tell them you've been over here," but she and I both knew that was what she meant.

I knew Momma and Daddy didn't like her, had felt them tense up whenever she was nearby. I'd never known them to speak a word to her, though she was our only close neighbor. They acted like Mrs. Winchester didn't even exist, like she was something dreamed up by a child's imagination.

A year passed before Momma caught on to what I was doing. One afternoon on the way home I found Momma waiting at the edge of the woods.

"Don't you never go see that old woman again," Momma hissed, like she was afraid Mrs. Winchester might hear.

Momma slipped through a gap in the barbed wire and pulled me behind her. I'd gotten my sleeve caught on the fence, but she didn't stop pulling, even when the cloth caught and made a tearing sound. You'd have thought there was a bull charging us.

After that Momma watched me like a hawk at home and at church. But by the next spring there was little reason to, because Mrs. Winchester's health had gotten bad. A mild stroke, Preacher Robertson called it, but it was enough to keep her from getting to church or out and about her yard.

So years passed, and I spoke not another word to Mrs. Winchester. Afternoons when the school bus went by her house I'd catch glimpses of her on the porch. I'd look out the window and see her staring toward the bus, toward me. I knew she searched through the glass for my face among all the others. And I somehow knew something else—that old and sick as she was she wouldn't die until I'd seen her again.

So when Sheriff Alexander came that Saturday and told me what he wanted, a part of me was surprised only that Mrs. Winchester had waited this long.

When I'd first glanced up and seen him coming down the field edge toward me, it might have been Daddy but for his uniform and hat. He moved slow like Daddy, with one leg stiff and dragging behind the other.

I wished it was Daddy. Field work had always seemed easier when we'd done it together. We could talk about school or baseball or how the crops were doing, and that would help pass the time.

Sheriff Alexander was a big man. You could see that even at a distance, tall and pussel-gutted, older than Daddy too. I looked up towards the house and saw the silver patrol car parked in the driveway. This ain't any good news coming my way, I thought.

"Isaac, isn't it?" Sheriff Alexander asked.

"Yes sir," I said, still on my knees.

Only when he spoke did I lay the butcher knife beside my sack. I didn't want to stop. I'd been cutting cabbage since dawn and I was wore out. I knew once I stopped it would be hard to get myself going again.

"They told us we had till 6:00 tomorrow," I said.

That was what the Carolina Power man had told Daddy the last time he'd come round, the same man who'd told us last winter not to plant anything, because there was a chance our part of the valley would flood before harvest time. But Daddy had told the Carolina Power man it was our land for a few more months yet, and he'd damn well do what he pleased.

Sheriff Alexander stepped closer, his shadow falling over me.

"I'm not here about that," he said.

He looked across the field, then back toward the house. "Your Daddy and Momma aren't here, are they?"

"No sir," I said. "They took the last of the furniture down to Seneca."

"Your daddy take a job down there?"

"He's working at Dobson Mill."

"So you all are living there now?"

"Yes sir. I'm just here to cut this cabbage."

Sheriff Alexander didn't say anything to that. He just stood there above me like he was listening for something. But the only sounds were the chain saws farther down the valley near Laurel Fork. He stared across the river at Licklog Mountain. The mountain had been scalped, mainly just stumps and rocks now. He looked up toward Crossroads Mountain and saw the same thing.

It was easy enough to guess what he was thinking, for like Daddy he'd grown up here. Though he'd left years ago I supposed it still bothered him to see it all changed.

"Momma and Daddy will be back to pick me up at five," I said, because his gaze was far-off, like he'd forgotten why he came.

"Maybe that's just as well," Sheriff Alexander said, looking at me now. "I came to see you. I've got a problem and you can help me."

I stood and dusted the dirt off my jeans. Whatever he wanted of me, I wanted to be level with him when I heard it.

"What kind of problem?"

"Your neighbor Mrs. Winchester. She says she won't leave until she talks to you. I'd just as soon not have to drag an old woman out of her house like she's a criminal, but if she doesn't come willingly I'll have no choice. That water's not waiting for anyone."

I looked toward the river and knew the truth of what he said. The tobacco was already underwater, and the land I stood on would soon be. I was in a race with the water to see who would get to the cabbage first.

"Are you going to help me, Isaac?"

I kept staring at the water, taking my time before I answered. I knew I was going to go see her, but a part of me wished I wasn't. I wanted to get the cabbage cut, get it all over with today and never have to come back.

I'd grown up knowing there was no future here, that Jocassee would sooner or later be covered in water, so I'd never let myself get attached to it the way Momma and Daddy had. I'd always known someday I'd have to leave. That's why I'd been in ROTC in high school instead of FFA and why I was headed to Clemson next fall on an ROTC scholarship.

"Why does she want to see me?" I asked, looking at eight rows of uncut cabbage.

"She didn't say. She just said she wasn't leaving until she did."

I looked at my watch. I could take off a few minutes and still get the cabbage cut by five.

"All right," I said.

I left the butcher knife and half-filled sack where they laid. We walked up to the house, Sheriff Alexander huffing and limping the whole way. I'd heard he'd been a good football player at one time, but he was in sorry shape now. It was easy to see why he wasn't running for sheriff again. He looked wore out, ready for checkers and a pair of bedroom slippers.

"I'll give you a ride," he said.

"I can walk over," I said. "Besides, I need to stop by the house a minute."

"I don't mind waiting," he said, so I just nodded.

I stepped into the house where I'd lived almost eighteen years, and it was like a building in one of those western ghost towns on television where the wind blows dust and tumbleweeds through empty streets.

Anything that would have made you believe people had lived here—chair, bed, TV, or picture—was gone. Daddy had even taken up bricks from the hearth. My steps echoed through the house, a lonely, empty sound. I walked into the room Daddy had added the year I was born. Something brown and clawed swooped past my head. It flapped down the hall and out the front door.

That gave my heart a jump start. It pounded so loud I could

hear the beating, or so it seemed, because everything else was so quiet and still. I went to the far corner of the room where my bed had been. Daddy had been a good farmer, but he wasn't quite as handy with a hammer and nails. A couple of the floor boards hadn't been nailed down good. When I was a kid I'd made a cubby hole under one of them.

I lifted the wood. Besides peppermints and sweet drinks, Mrs. Winchester had given me one other thing when I was a kid, something I'd forgotten until Sheriff Alexander's visit reminded me. I rooted my hand in the space under the board. I brought up a couple of arrowheads and buffalo nickels before I found what I was searching for.

I looked around the room a last time. I'd slept in another house a month, but mornings when I woke there was always a moment I expected to see these walls, to see the sun slanting in through these windows. I was learning that leaving a place wasn't as easy as packing up and getting out. You carried part of it with you, whether you wanted to or not.

We didn't talk on the way over to Mrs. Winchester's, but the radio was on, Johnny Cash singing "I Walk the Line." I tuned it out and thought about what it would be like to live in a dorm next fall with a bunch of people my own age. It figured to be quite an adjustment, especially since I'd had no brothers or sisters. I wondered if even at Clemson there would be times I'd wake up and think for a moment I was still up here.

I bet there would be, and I bet there'd be times I'd be lonesome or worried about passing a course and wish I was back bedding tobacco with Daddy or sitting down to Momma's biscuits and gravy. Every kid leaving home feels this way, I told myself—excited but a little scared too.

Sheriff Alexander cut off the radio when we pulled in behind the hulk of rusted metal now more lattice than truck. Creeper, honeysuckle and the trumpet vines Daddy called cow's itch covered the metal like a green net. Orange flowers blossomed from the trumpet vines.

Sheriff Alexander glanced at his watch.

"I've got to go see my brother," he said. "He's as stubborn about leaving as that old woman. You tell Mrs. Winchester she's got thirty minutes to talk to you and get together what she's taking to the nursing home. You tell her even if she's not ready we're going anyway. I've got to get her down to Seneca and myself back up here. I've plenty enough other things besides her to deal with today."

I opened the car door.

"Thirty minutes," Sheriff Alexander said.

I smelled kerosene as I stepped on the porch. The door was open, so I walked in, the front room dark as a movie theatre, the kerosene fumes so thick it was more like breathing water than air. Quilts and blankets and balled-up pages of newspaper covered the front room's floor, all of it reeking of kerosene.

I heard a ticking sound and looked at the clock, its hands still where they'd been a decade ago. Kerosene dripped off the fire-board and onto the hearth like time itself leaked from the clock's base.

Mrs. Winchester stood in front of the fireplace. She wore a black cotton dress. A Sunday-go-to-meeting dress, Momma would call it. She held a five-gallon steel can in her right hand. I crossed the room and took it from her. Nothing sloshed in the bottom. She'd poured out every drop.

"I'll not allow that lake to cover up this house," she said. "I'll burn it to the ground first."

Mrs. Winchester's words were slurred, the left side of her face froze like a mask. Her right hand reached up to the fire-board where the picture of her youngest son stared down at us, but it wasn't the picture she took from the mantle. It was a box of kitchen matches. I took them from her.

"You can't do that," I told her, though I had no idea why not.

"Let's go out on the porch," I said, because the kerosene fumes gave me a headache. I took her by the arm and led her out of the gloomy house and into the light. It was cool for late September. The radio had claimed we might have our first frost come morning. I asked her if she wanted me to get her coat, but she shook her head. She sat in the rocker, and I perched myself beside her on the railing.

I stuffed the matches in my front pocket. As I did my fingertip jabbed against the Gold Star.

"Here, before I forget," I said, pulling the medal out of my pocket. "I brought this for you."

I held the Gold Star out to her.

"That there belongs to you, not me," she said.

"I think you ought to keep it now," I said.

She reached out her right hand then, but she didn't take what I offered. Her cold, veiny hand curled my fingers back over my palm. Her hand pressed mine into a fist, and she didn't let go, her grip stronger than I would have thought for a woman that old. I almost lost my balance, reached with my free hand to grip the railing as I felt the Gold Star's points break my skin and dampen my palm with blood. Mrs. Winchester squeezed my hand harder. A blood drop fell on the gray wood under our hands. The stain it made was no bigger round than a piece of double-00 buckshot, but it was enough to make her let my hand go. I stuffed the Gold Star back in my jeans.

"He wanted you to have it," she said, the words slurred enough to make me think maybe I hadn't heard her right.

It made no sense, her saying "he" when her son hadn't even known me.

"He?"

"Holland," she said, like that would clear it up. Her brown eyes looked deep into mine now. The side of her face that wasn't froze twitched like a current ran under her skin.

I gripped the railing with both hands. Whatever she'd been

waiting to tell me all this time, I knew she couldn't hold it inside any longer. It was like my mind was trying to beat her to it, because I was bringing up things from the past that connected me to that soldier above the fireplace.

What my mind grabbed on was what she'd said years ago about me looking like her son. She wasn't the only one who'd noticed such a thing.

"You're a Winchester, aren't you?" Mr. Pipkin had said the first day I'd walked into my eighth grade home room. The way he'd spoke made it clear he didn't much like the idea I might be.

"No sir," I said. "I'm a Holcombe."

"Then your Momma must be," Mr. Pipkin had said.

"No sir. She was a Boone."

But Mr. Pipkin had looked at me like he thought I was lying, and he'd held a grudge against me from that first day to the end of the school year.

"He wanted you to have it," Mrs. Winchester said again, like maybe I hadn't heard her the first time.

"Why?"

The smell of kerosene filled the porch now as if it had soaked through the walls. Mrs. Winchester's eyes met mine, and it was that same hungry look she'd had in church when I was four years old.

"Because you're his son."

When she said that it didn't matter that I gripped the railing with both hands, because it was like the wood I sat on no longer connected to the porch or anything else. It was like that moment on a swing when your outstretched legs and feet reach out over your head. For a second you're suspended in midair, defying gravity, and your hands grip the ropes even tighter, because you know you're about to fall.

But there were no ropes for me to hold on to.

"I don't believe that," I said.

"Don't believe me," she said. "Believe your own eyes."

She nodded at the door.

"Go back in yonder and study that picture. Look at it good. Even if you won't hear the truth you'll see it."

I didn't move, probably couldn't have moved if I'd wanted to. My mind brought up all sorts of memories, each one like a piece of a puzzle being put together. I remembered how at family get-togethers my relatives sometimes remarked to Momma and Daddy about my brown eyes, how rare they were in the family, and it was kin on both sides saying that.

I remembered how Momma and Daddy had always tried to keep me away from Mrs. Winchester, how Momma had dragged me through the barbed wire and back onto our land that morning she'd caught me leaving Mrs. Winchester's house. There were other things, like me being an only child, and the way Daddy had sometimes looked at me, almost like he saw something that made him afraid. It seemed every second my mind dredged up something else.

I no longer felt like I was hanging in midair. I was falling now and I hoped I'd hit so hard I'd knock myself out, because I didn't want to remember anything else. Mrs. Winchester reached out and grabbed my wrist, like she'd read my mind and feared I'd tumble right off the porch.

"If there was ever another way I'd have not told you," she said, still gripping my wrist, "for you'll have burdens enough in your life without this. But you're the only one that can do what's got to be done. You're the only one that can get them to tell you where your real daddy is."

"I don't understand," I said.

The kerosene fumes were so thick now it was like we were underwater. My head pounded and my eyes watered. I felt like I was drowning.

"Your real daddy," she said. "Them that raised you know

where he is."

"He's alive?"

"No, he ain't alive."

This must be a dream, I told myself, because that's exactly what it felt like all of a sudden—a dream where everything seems real then suddenly nothing at all makes sense. Open your eyes and you'll see you're in bed, I told myself. I blinked but nothing happened. I was still on the front porch and Mrs. Winchester was still in her chair beside me, her cold hand clamped like iron around my wrist.

"You don't know where he is?"

"No," she said.

"Then why would Momma and Daddy know?"

"Because they killed him."

Suddenly the wood I sat on was nailed solid to the porch again, the world firm under my feet. Maybe the stroke has done this to her, I thought. Maybe she's just old and addled. When I freed my hand from her wrist, I felt bony fingers that didn't want to let go of me.

You really had me going for a minute, old woman, I thought. Had me believing all sorts of nonsense.

"You don't believe me," she said.

"No," I said, but I wasn't looking at her. I was looking down the road for the sheriff. I wanted to leave, not just her porch but Jocassee. I wanted to get back in the field and cut the rest of the cabbage. Then I'd be free of this place and her along with it once and for all.

"Don't believe me," she said. "Believe your momma. Show her that Gold Star. Ask what she and that man of hers done to your real daddy."

I heard the patrol car coming up the road, and I lifted myself off the railing. Her hand reached out and grabbed my wrist again.

"You can't let that lake cover up your daddy's bones," she said, her voice trembling now. "The dead can't have no peace till they is proper buried. You find your daddy, boy. You don't let that lake cover him up. You got to do that for him. You're the only one who can."

The sheriff pulled up behind the truck.

"Leave me alone," I said, and yanked my arm free. I stepped off the porch.

"You're the only one," she said again, but I didn't turn around.

Sheriff Alexander didn't look very happy. You could tell his visit had gone no better than mine.

"I'm going back to the field," I said.

"I can give you a ride."

"No, it's not far if I cut through the woods."

"Suit yourself," Sheriff Alexander said. "You all have a good conversation?"

The way he said it I could tell he was curious and wanted to know what had passed between me and Mrs. Winchester.

"Not really," I said.

That didn't satisfy Sheriff Alexander.

"What did she want?" he said, and he said it like I was some kind of suspect he was questioning.

"Nothing. She was just babbling. She's crazy, Sheriff. She was getting ready to set her house on fire."

I pulled the kitchen matches from my pocket.

"These are hers."

Sheriff Alexander took the matches and looked up at the porch where Mrs. Winchester stood. She made no move to join us. Feel sorry for her, I told myself. She was good to you when you were a kid. She can't help being old and addled.

"Let's go, Mrs. Winchester," Sheriff Alexander said.

"Let me get my grip," she said and went into the house.

She closed the door behind her out of habit, like she was going to be in there a while, like she had a fire going inside and didn't want the September morning to chill a house that was warm and cozy.

But she didn't have a fire. Not yet.

"What?" Sheriff Alexander said, but I was already running toward the porch.

When I reached the first step I heard a whoosh, and yellow flames climbed the shades behind the windows. I twisted the door knob, but it wouldn't turn. I could hear crackling and popping now. I rammed my shoulder against the door. It wouldn't give. Then the sheriff was beside me. On the third try we broke the door down.

She sat in the middle of the room, flames rising right out of her lap and blooming across her chest. Her hair was a tangle of fire. She was like those monks in Vietnam I'd seen on TV, because she wasn't screaming or crying or trying to put out the flames. She just sat there dying.

"Don't try," the sheriff said, but I was already running through the flames. I dragged Mrs. Winchester toward the door, my hands gripping her arms. Skin flaked off her like charred paper. A smell stronger than kerosene made me gag.

Sheriff Alexander helped me get her into the yard. We rolled her body to douse the flames. That was all it was now, a body.

"She's dead, ain't she," I said.

Sheriff Alexander pressed his finger against what little flesh hung on her wrist.

"For her sake I hope so," he said.

"Mrs. Winchester?" I said, looking at her face.

But she had no ears to hear me. They had been burned off along with her eyebrows and hair. The only thing on her face that still looked human was her eyes. They were open and staring right at me.

"No pulse," Sheriff Alexander said, letting go of her wrist.

He grunted and stood up. He winced and rubbed his knee. He looked at the house, what was left of it. Then he looked at me.

"You're burned," he said.

I looked at my hands.

"It ain't bad," I said.

"I've got to call an ambulance," Sheriff Alexander said. "A fire truck too, I guess, though it doesn't look likely to spread."

"What can I do?" I asked.

"Nothing. You did what you could. This is what she wanted, to die here where she lived her whole life. I can understand that."

"But it's an awful way to die," I said.

"No more awful for her than being taken away from the only place she's ever known," Sheriff Alexander said, his voice cold and harsh. "She'd have lasted a month at most in that nursing home. If you could ask her now, I'd bet she'd tell you she was glad she did it."

My eyes watered, but it was no longer from the kerosene. I looked at the burning house instead of Sheriff Alexander. I didn't want to look into his eyes, eyes that had seen too much. This must be the way you get when your job is to deal with the terrible things that happen to people, I thought. A farmer gets calluses on his hands. A sheriff gets them on his heart.

"Can't you at least cover her?"

"I've got a blanket in the trunk," Sheriff Alexander said. "If you want to do something, you can put it on her while I call this in."

I did what he asked. As I lay the blanket over Mrs. Winchester I looked into her eyes a last time, eyes that had watched me all my life, eyes the same dark brown as mine.

"You're a Winchester, aren't you," Mr. Pipkin had said.

I wondered if I was the one that was crazy, because suddenly what she'd told me, part of it at least, seemed not only possible but certain. It was like I was believing one thing one minute and something the exact opposite the next. You're just upset, I told myself. What you've just seen would make anybody crazy for a while.

But Mr. Pipkin hadn't been crazy. He'd been a mean old man but he hadn't been crazy. Neither had my kinfolk when they took note of my eyes.

Sheriff Alexander finished his call. He stared at where the house had been. There were only a few flames now, no bigger than campfires.

"I've never seen anything burn that fast," Sheriff Alexander said. "She must have planned that fire for weeks."

"I'm leaving now," I told him.

"I'd drive you," he said, "but it's best I stay and make sure this fire doesn't flare back up." He turned toward me, his voice softer.

"I'm truly sorry you had to see this, son."

I stepped into the woods and then over the few sagging strands of barbed wire that hadn't rusted completely away. I looked a last time at the smoke and ashes that had once been a house, at a blanket that covered what had once been a person.

"You feel things deeper than most people," Momma had said years back when I'd come home from school crying. "That ought to be a blessing but it ain't."

Maybe Momma was right, because what I felt was deep inside me, so deep I couldn't bring it out enough to give it words.

There was still cabbage to cut, but I walked on past where my butcher knife and sack laid. It felt like years had passed since I'd been kneeling in that field. That cabbage didn't seem of much importance now.

I followed the river downstream, not really knowing where I was going. It was like my mind moved so fast it was taking my body right along with it. Soon the river path was underwater. I climbed uphill and found an old hunting trail.

Part of what she'd said, the part about Momma and Daddy killing her son, I couldn't have believed in a million years. It was so crazy it made me want to laugh out loud. Maybe that's what grief does to you, I thought. Her saying that makes the rest of it a lie, shouldn't it? Yes, it should, I thought, but does it?

I suddenly wished a terrible thing. I wished Mrs. Winchester had killed herself yesterday or last week or anytime before this morning, before she'd had a chance to talk to me. I reached into my pocket and took out the Gold Star. I could fling it in the river and be done with it, be done with everything she'd told me that morning. I reared my arm back but I couldn't do it. I put the Gold Star back in my pocket and walked on down the trail to where the gorge opened up.

What had once been a meadow with a river running through it now looked like a low-country swamp. Scrub pines and blackjack oaks the loggers hadn't bothered with rose out of the water. The stumps of the big hardwoods jutted out like tombstones. But the farther you went the less you saw. Water deepened and hid more. At the end of the valley where the mountains again came close together, a white wall of concrete cut off the river like a tourniquet cuts off a vein.

I looked across the water to the cemetery on Matthews Ridge. You could see where the gravestones had been rooted up. It looked like somebody had been digging for treasure.

I thought about last Monday when me and Daddy had crossed the river and seen those gravestones taken up.

Momma hadn't wanted to go. She said it would be an awful sight and wanted no part of it, but Daddy had felt obliged to be there since it was some of his people being moved.

"I couldn't rest easy without knowing it's done with some respect," Daddy had said.

Daddy hadn't asked me to go. I could tell he'd just as soon I'd stayed at the house with Momma. But I went anyway, as much out of curiosity as anything.

Sheriff Alexander and Mr. Pearson watched from outside the back fence as the work crew got started, the machinery snarling and grunting as it rolled right over the front gate.

"They ought not to have done that," Daddy said, but I couldn't see how it much mattered. Soon enough there'd be nothing for that fence to keep in or out. Daddy and I walked over to where the sheriff and Mr. Pearson stood, Sheriff Alexander wearing his gray uniform and Mr. Pearson his black suit.

There wasn't much talk among us, maybe because nobody knew exactly how we should feel about what was happening. It wasn't a funeral but it wasn't something to feel good about either. Mr. Pearson wore his best poker face. Daddy looked grim. Sheriff Alexander looked grim too, grim but also angry.

"We're just moving the stones today," Mr. Pearson told Daddy. "I still got the graves at Tamassee Grove to dig before I do these. That way we can rebury the same day."

Daddy looked relieved to hear that. He felt the need to be here, but it wasn't something he'd wanted to do. He was more than willing to put off the raising of his own daddy and momma a few more days.

The backhoe and tripod made quick work of it, yanking the gravestones out of the ground like teeth, so it wasn't long before the tripod brought up the stone that had JACOB HOLCOMBE and SUSANNA HOLCOMBE chiseled in it. I read the dates as the names rose in the air. BORN JUNE 8, 1899 DIED DECEMBER 1, 1955. BORN APRIL 5, 1904 DIED MARCH 21, 1964. Beneath that REST IN PEACE. The tripod lowered the stone into the truck. I looked at Daddy. His face had got pale and he gripped the fence like he feared he was about to be swept away by something. He wasn't looking at the stone. He was looking at the grave. Nightcrawlers big around as cigarettes wiggled in the black gash where the stone had been.

Mr. Pearson had been watching Daddy too. He came over to do what he'd been doing for people most of his life. He put his arm on Daddy's shoulder and asked Daddy if he wanted to sit in the hearse until he felt better.

"No," Daddy said. "I'm going to the house. I can't watch this no more."

But Daddy didn't move. He just shut his eyes and held on to the fence a while longer.

"This is wrong, Melvin," Sheriff Alexander said. "You know it's wrong."

"I don't like it any more than you, but there's no choice," Mr. Pearson said. "It's a federal law. Besides, if we don't move these coffins they'll come up on their own. There's oxygen trapped in them. They'll come bobbing up like fishing corks soon as the ground gets saturated. Is that what you want?"

Sheriff Alexander didn't answer. His gray eyes got hard and cold as flint. He wasn't looking at Mr. Pearson or me or Daddy or anyone else. He was thinking about something, and whatever it was it gave him no pleasure.

"Let's go," Daddy had said, and we'd gone back across the river.

Now, four days later as I stared across the water at the cemetery, I remembered something else, a small thing I'd forgotten soon as it was said, forgotten until Mrs. Winchester had started my mind digging up all sorts of things—though nothing solid as a granite tombstone, not yet at least.

What I remembered was what Sheriff Alexander had said when he'd seen me with Daddy at the cemetery.

"This your boy?" he'd asked Daddy.

"Yes," Daddy had said, but Sheriff Alexander had looked like he hadn't believed it. He looked at me like he'd seen me before and was trying to remember where. He'd looked at me the same way Mr. Pipkin had that first day of school.

"Show that Gold Star to your momma," Mrs. Winchester had said, and I knew now that I would. It wasn't something I wanted to do but I knew I'd have to do it, because the not knowing was worse than the knowing. At least that's what I told myself.

Now even the hunting trail was underwater, so I climbed up the ridge and walked toward where the mountains again rubbed up close to one another and the dam sealed the valley. Chain saws rattled far off on the other side of the water, but otherwise it was quiet, so quiet you could almost believe water had already risen over everything.

I looked at my watch. I had three more hours before Momma and the man who claimed to be my daddy came and picked me up. He'd be fussing about the cabbage not being cut, but that was the least thing bothering me now.

I was in the shadow of the dam when I saw the white Carolina Power truck. I turned around. I didn't want to have to talk to anyone.

"What are you doing up here, boy?" a voice said.

I kept on walking but in a few seconds I could hear him coming through the woods.

"I asked you a question, boy," he said when he caught up with me. He grabbed my shoulder and turned me.

I looked at him then. He wore a yellow hard hat—the flimsy, plastic kind that look plain stupid on someone wearing a dress shirt and tie. A name tag with SHERMAN JAMESON—ENGINEER printed on it dangled from his shirt pocket.

"I've been cutting cabbage," I said. "I'm taking a little break before I finish up."

"What's your name?"

For a second I paused, not sure what my name was.

"Isaac," I said, leaving it at that.

"Well, you're trespassing."

He said it in a pissed-off way.

"You all said we had till tomorrow."

"That's changed. Some old woman getting evicted set herself on fire. That kind of thing is bad public relations, and we're not going to risk something else like that. We've got enough problems dealing with the archaeologists and bird watchers. Everybody's out of this valley today."

"What does Sheriff Alexander say?"

"It's not up to him to say a damn thing. All he's done is get in our way. It was him that talked us into letting you people stay long as you have."

He nodded up at the dam.

"But none of that matters anymore. It doesn't matter how many Indian mounds are here or what flowers or bugs or birds. If you found chunks of gold big as baseballs it wouldn't matter now. That dam's built, and the gates are closed. It doesn't matter if you're living or dead. You don't belong here anymore. Every last one of you hillbillies is going to be flushed out of this valley like shit down a commode."

You're wrong about that, I thought, at least about the dead, because I'd stumbled across graves while rabbit hunting. There'd be nothing more than a clearing in the woods and a few creek stones with whatever name had been scratched on it long gone. Nobody had dug up those graves. Nobody had dug up the grave at the head of Wolf Creek either, a grave with no marker, a grave some people claimed held a witch.

A coon hunter had found her dead in the woods when I was eight. Daddy and a couple of other men buried her in the woods behind her house. They'd built a coffin out of cedar wood, because cedar won't rot. They hadn't done it to keep the dirt and water out. They'd done it to keep her in.

I saw no reason to tell Sherman Jameson any of this though. I turned and started walking back to what was left of the farm. I waited for his hand to reach out and grab my shoulder again but it didn't. Which was a good thing for him. If he had I would have laid him flat on his back.

"Don't come back tomorrow," he said. "If you do you'll be

arrested."

I didn't look back but I could feel the dam looming behind me as if it cast a shadow over the whole valley. I stepped over a crumbling stone fence. The Gold Star jabbed my leg through the denim. The water hadn't risen fast enough, I thought. It should have come like a flood and washed us all out so quick there wouldn't have been time for secrets that had been long hid in this valley to be revealed, secrets that should have been buried under this lake forever. Because it was like the last few hours I had been trying to walk away from the truth I saw in my own eyes but the truth had been trailing me like a bloodhound. Now it had a hold on me and wouldn't let go.

When I got back to the house, I sat on the steps. My sandwich was in a paper bag on the porch, but I had no appetite. The farm seemed different from when I'd left it in the morning, like the earth had somehow moved under it and shifted everything—fields, barn, shed, and house—a few yards from where things had been before.

Maybe this wasn't ever your home, I told myself. Maybe somewhere else is your real home. Maybe your real father isn't dead, just the part about him being murdered by people who raised you a lie. Or maybe it is all a lie. One second I believed one thing, and the next I believed just the opposite.

I didn't move from those steps till they drove up.

"Why ain't you finished?" he asked.

"I got tired."

He looked put out with me.

"Sheriff Alexander's done set up a roadblock. He says we can't come back tomorrow."

He looked at the rows of uncut cabbage.

"Damn, son, that's a sure ten dollars we could have used."

"Billy," Momma said, and she said it sharp.

His voice softened.

"The sheriff said you was there when Mrs. Winchester got

burned."

"Yes, I was there," I said, not meeting his eyes.

"I'm sorry you were," Daddy said. "I reckon seeing such would take the starch out of most anyone. Don't you fret none about that cabbage, son. I shouldn't have spoke ever a thing about it."

"We better get going," Momma said. "Sheriff Alexander told us not to tarry."

We got in the truck but he didn't crank the engine. He and Momma stared through the glass at the farm. For the last time, I suddenly realized. Any other day I would have tried to say something to make them feel better.

But not this day.

"It's a pretty place," Momma said. "I don't notion I knew how pretty till these last few days."

"But it won't be much longer," he said, but in a soft way.

"That's the worst thing," Momma said. "Even if I never laid eyes on this valley again, there'd be a comfort in knowing it would stay the way I'd always known it, not buried under a lake."

They stared a while out the window, maybe trying to freeze it in their minds so they'd never forget.

"We best be going," he finally said. "There's nothing for us here anymore."

The truck bumped down the drive. Momma kept looking back, even when we got on the road. It was like she expected the farm to disappear the second she took her eyes off it.

We passed Mrs. Winchester's mailbox. The ground where the house had been looked like someone had spread a black quilt over it. All that was left was the brick chimney and tin roof. That and a few wisps of smoke. I could feel Momma and him tense as we passed by. I wondered if Sheriff Alexander had told them Mrs. Winchester had talked to me.

The road curved away from the river. The sun had fallen

behind Sassafras Mountain, and the woods were shadowy. The air had a chill to it.

"There'll come a hard frost tonight," he said.

He said it without thinking, talking more to himself than to Momma and me, because it was a natural thing for him to take notice of, natural as smelling rain coming or spotting blue mold on a tobacco leaf. He'd been a mill worker for months but a farmer for decades.

"What on earth," Momma said as the road straightened out, because two police cars and a white Carolina Power truck were parked in Travis Alexander's front yard.

The sheriff stood on the front porch, his deputy and the Carolina Power man I'd seen earlier that afternoon beside him. Travis Alexander stood on the porch too, his hands clasped in front of him like a man praying. He wasn't talking to God though. He was cussing, some of his words shouted at the engineer but most at his brother as Sheriff Alexander put his hand on Travis's arm and helped him down the steps and into the back seat of the patrol car.

"Lord help us," Momma said. "What awful thing more can happen in this valley."

~

I didn't change into my pajamas that night, just took off my boots and laid down on my bed in my jeans and denim work shirt. I knew I wasn't going to be doing much sleeping. Instead I'd be thinking, searching for the words I'd speak come morning, words that would have to be chose careful to get me to the truth of what I had to know.

But I had all night. I wanted a little time before I searched for those words. I turned on the radio, because sometimes music can take you out of yourself when you're bothered. I found some good music—Allman Brothers, Creedence Clearwater—but it might just as well have been dentist chair music for all the attention my mind paid to it.

I cut off the radio and stared at the ceiling. I didn't want to close my eyes, because I knew soon as I did I'd see Mrs. Winchester sitting on the floor, flames rising from her lap like something she was cradling.

After a while I cut off the light. An ambulance wailed out on the by-pass. Someone across the street slammed a front door, a car passed a few yards from my window. All town noises none of us had gotten used to.

"We'll rent a few months and then get us a place out in the country," he'd said after we moved in.

"It can't be soon enough for me," Momma had said. "I don't see how anyone gets any sleep with such racket all hours of the night."

I started putting words together in my mind and then erasing them. It was like I was doing a crossword. Every word had to fit in a certain place. But they didn't fit, no matter how many times I scrambled them up. She'd lied to me almost eighteen years, so she was good at it. The words I wanted would hit Momma so fast and hard her face couldn't help but show the truth right then and there.

The newspaper thumped on the driveway across the street before I knew what I was going to do. It was a simple thing, so simple I shouldn't have taken a whole night to figure it out. I wouldn't even need words, at least not at first.

I slept then, maybe just a few minutes, maybe an hour, but when I woke I smelled coffee.

For a few moments it was like I'd completely forgotten yesterday—Daddy and Momma were who they'd always been, Mrs. Winchester was alive and whatever secrets she had she kept to herself. Then I felt the Gold Star pricking my skin like a briar. I got out of bed and laced up my boots. I took the Gold Star from my pocket and closed my hand over it. I took a deep breath and walked into the kitchen.

Momma was putting the milk in the refrigerator. I waited for her to turn around. When she did I opened my palm.

I'd done the right thing, because her face told me more than any words. She pressed her back against the refrigerator, almost like I held a spider or snake in my hand.

"Mrs. Winchester gave it to me," I said. "She told me you know where my father is. Where is he, Momma?"

"Oh, God," Momma said. She sagged like I'd punched her in the stomach. She put her hands over her face like she was trying to hide what part of her she could.

"Tell me, Momma," I said. Then I said the thing I didn't believe. "She says you killed him, Momma."

"Your momma didn't kill him. I did."

He stood in the doorway, bare-chested, shaving cream covering his face like a fake beard.

"Don't say it, Billy," Momma said.

"Where is he buried?"

The words came from me, but it was like they came from another person's mouth, somebody I didn't know any better than I knew the two strangers listening to those words. This is a dream. It has to be. Open your eyes, I told myself.

But my eyes were already open.

"That old woman told you a passel of lies," Momma said, like my ears hadn't just heard him say it was all true. "We don't know nothing of what she told you. She was a crazy old woman. She was liable to tell you most anything."

"Where is he buried?" I said again, but I wasn't looking at Momma anymore. I was staring at the man who stood in the doorway.

"A lie will always find you out," he'd once told me years ago. Whether he believed it then I reckoned he believed it now. He looked me dead in the eyes. Whatever he was going to say would be the truth.

"The side of Licklog facing the river. Next to a big ash tree."

"She told me I couldn't let that water cover him up," I said, the words still like someone else's words. Maybe they always would be, I thought, because maybe the person I had been no longer existed.

"She lied," Momma whispered.

"He ain't going to stay down in that valley and be covered up," I said, still looking at him. "You're going to show me where he is."

"Yes," he said. "I know."

"Don't, Billy," Momma said. She was crying now.

Then she looked at me.

"Don't believe it, son," she said. "Don't believe it even if it's true."

She reached her arms out to me, but I stepped away.

"Don't go back there," she said. "Let that lake cover it all up, son—the good and the bad."

"He can't do that, Amy," he said.

"Put the shovels in the truck," he said to me. "I'll get dressed and be out there in a minute."

It was strange how he said it, so calm and matter-of-fact, like we were going to go dig up some redworms for fishing. Maybe he's trying to trick me, I thought. Maybe he's going to go out the back door and disappear. How could you know what a stranger might do?

Except he wasn't a stranger, and telling myself he was didn't change things a whit. I knew him, even now, knew him well enough to know he wasn't going to run.

I stood there and waited. He came out of the bedroom dressed in his farming clothes, the clothes Momma had put in the bottom drawer once he'd started work at the mill. He'd wiped off the shaving cream. I could see his face, and despite all that had happened it was a face I knew.

"Let's go," he said.

He looked at Momma.

"You staying here?"

"No," Momma said. "I'm going."

It seemed like I was one of the astronauts walking on the moon. Each step I took seemed in slow motion. It was like everything I had ever known, even how to walk, was uncertain now. I got two shovels and threw them in the back of the truck with the cabbage sacks I hadn't filled. They came out in a minute, her pulling on a sweater while he locked the door.

"Give me the keys," I said. "I'm driving."

He did what I told him. I cranked the engine and drove out of Seneca, making one more trip back to Jocassee than I'd planned.

I drove fast, faster than I should have because the roads were slick with rain. The windshield wipers made their tick-tock sound, and it seemed a reminder of time running out. Carolina Power had said it would take ten more months for the lake to fill up, but in my mind it was like I was racing water rising by the second.

"It ain't already underwater, is it?" I asked.

"That's not likely," he said. "It's high ground."

"We can't do this," Momma said. "It's too late, years too late," but it was like she was talking to herself.

It wasn't like a dream anymore. What I felt was just the opposite, like everything in my life had been a long, deep dream till I opened my hand and showed Momma the Gold Star. It was like I had just been born and was seeing the world for the first time. What I was seeing and hearing could have made me cry like a newborn baby. But it didn't. There was a coldness in my heart that kept any tears froze deep inside me. We listened to the windshield wipers as we headed up into the mountains, the sky above us gray and low.

I turned off the blacktop and onto the dirt road. The road curved and dropped. I braked and jerked the steering wheel to keep us on the road.

"Slow down, son," he said.

But I wasn't going to slow down. I bumped and swerved on

down the road, not much caring if I ran off or not.

Then I came out of a curve and saw the roadblock laid in the middle of the road like a giant sawhorse, the silver patrol car parked on the left edge of the road. Sheriff Alexander looked right at me through the windshield as I swerved to the right side. I ran two wheels into the ditch and clipped the roadblock. I swerved back onto the road and kept going, past Travis Alexander's farm, then Mrs. Winchester's before turning, leaving the road where the mailbox said Holcombe.

I didn't go all the way up the drive. I scraped and bucked over the ditch and into the cabbage field I hadn't harvested. I didn't stop until I came to water.

I got out and took a shovel from the truck bed.

"We'll need this too," he said, and handed me a cabbage sack.

That's when I realized what should have been clear from the start. What we were going to find wasn't going to be in a coffin. Murderers didn't put their victims in coffins.

Sheriff Alexander's car came up the drive. He slowed for a second in front of the house, then bumped down the field edge and parked twenty yards from the truck. He didn't try to drive through the field. Unlike me he was worried about getting out of there.

"What in the hell are you all doing?" Sheriff Alexander said as he limped toward us.

"What should have been done a long time ago, Sheriff," he said. "What can't be hid no longer."

"And what's that, Billy?" Sheriff Alexander asked.

"Holland Winchester. The man I killed."

Sheriff Alexander stopped like he'd been hit by a two by four. He stood there not ten yards from us. It seemed he couldn't take another step. His weight made his shoes sink deeper in the mud, almost like he was taking root in the ground.

"You can handcuff me if you want," he said, holding his hands out to Sheriff Alexander. "But I ain't going to run. I never figured to do that, even in the worst of it."

Sheriff Alexander didn't move and neither did any of the rest of us. We just stood there with the rain dripping off us like statues on a courthouse lawn.

"It's too late, Billy," Sheriff Alexander finally said. His voice was gentle, a gentleness you wouldn't think such a big man would have in him, especially after all the meanness he'd seen as a law man.

He stepped toward us, his shoes squishing as he pulled them out of the mud.

"Let's get out of here, Billy. Whatever's been done has been done. We're too old to change it now. Let the water cover it up."

"I got to do it, Sheriff," he said and lifted the other shovel from the truck bed.

"What about you?" Sheriff Alexander said to Momma. "Surely you've got enough sense to know I'm right."

Momma looked at Sheriff Alexander and then she looked at us. It was like she wasn't sure whose side she was on.

"It's got to be done," she finally said.

Sheriff Alexander shook his head like he was put out with all three of us. He took his glasses off and wiped the rain from the lenses. He was thinking about what he was going to say, what he was going to do. His gray eyes looked beyond tired, like they'd seen more than they could bear the last few days and their grayness was nothing but smoke left over from something snuffed out. You could tell he hadn't slept much last night. I wondered if it was what had happened with Mrs. Winchester or what had happened with his brother that had kept him awake and drained the light from his eyes.

"Where is he?" Sheriff Alexander asked as he put his glasses back on.

"Across the river," I said.

Sheriff Alexander looked at the water that covered the lower part of the field. His eyes followed it across the river bed and to the foot of Licklog.

"This isn't going to be easy. That river's deeper now."

"You don't have to go," I said.

It was raining steady now, and the clouds promised it would only get harder. I stepped into the water.

"I'm going, son," Sheriff Alexander said, his voice angry. "But I'm getting a rope out of my trunk first. I don't want someone to drown doing this, so you just wait a damn minute."

Sheriff Alexander walked over to the patrol car and got a rope, but not before talking on his radio.

"You lead," he said, handing me a rope end.

I picked up the shovel and cabbage sack with my free hand. I stepped into the water, the rope straightening out behind me.

"You next, Billy," Sheriff Alexander said.

"I'm going too," Momma said, reaching out for the rope as well.

No one argued with her. Sheriff Alexander grabbed the other rope end and wrapped it around his hand like I'd done.

"I'll carry that shovel, Billy," Sheriff Alexander said. "You just worry with holding on to that rope."

The water barely covered my boots at first. I was still in the field, or what until a few days ago had been a field. It was like slogging through a black-water swamp, for the mud hid the limbs and trees the loggers had left. I stumbled twice before I'd even got out of the field. I could feel the others behind me, the rope tightening and tugging each time they stumbled or paused. I glanced back and it was a sorry-looking sight. The rain had drenched their clothes, and they hung onto the rope like shipwreck survivors. They'll never make it, I thought. I'll end up crossing this river alone.

Beyond the field the going got easier despite the current. The river ran dingy from the rain, but unlike in the fields you could make out the bottom. I found the shallows below a blue hole and started across. I took my time, looking for patches of white sand between the trees and limbs and rocks. The water rose to my kneecaps but no higher.

I didn't know I was across until I bumped against the bank. I half-stepped and half-crawled to where the water got swampy and still again, but not before I'd slipped and slid back down the bank a couple of times. It was a hard thing to do without dropping the shovel or cabbage sack.

I pulled the others up the bank.

"That river's rising," Sheriff Alexander said. "This needs to be done fast."

Sheriff Alexander handed the shovel to him.

"This way," he said, not waiting for Sheriff Alexander to finish looping the rope. He led us through the shallow water, using the shovel like a cane to keep his balance when he stumbled.

We started up Licklog. The rain came harder now, a cold rain, the kind that soaked to your bones. We were all shivering and miserable, not a stitch of dry clothing among us. The clouds looked low enough to touch.

"Here," he said. "It's right around here."

He stepped around the stumps, trying to find the one that belonged to the ash tree. Then he stopped.

"This is it," he said, standing in a clear spot. He held out the shovel and moved it over the ground like a dowsing stick.

"Somewhere right in here," he said.

He dug on one side and I started on the other. The rain had made the ground soft so it was easy going, easy enough to where my thoughts could go where they wanted. That wasn't such a good thing. My mind was tangled as a blackberry patch and it seemed to be getting more tangled by the minute. An hour ago I'd wanted to believe there was only one way I could feel about the man beside me but that had just been wishful thinking on my part. We'd shared too much.

Even now we worked together, side by side, the same way we'd done my whole life. My deepest memory—deeper than Mrs. Winchester's eyes on me at church, deeper than Momma rocking me when an earache wouldn't let me sleep—was being with him in the fields, a jar of pretty-colored potato bugs in my hand. Helping him, or at least that's what he told me those days I followed him through the fields.

Think of something bad he did to you, I told myself. But there wasn't anything. He'd never raised his hand against me or cussed me. He'd punished me when I'd deserved it but ever always in a gentle way. My not being his son hadn't stopped him from loving me like a son.

The rain suddenly came harder, like a big knife had slit the sky open. I couldn't see but a few feet in any direction. It was like a white curtain had fell around us, shutting off the rest of the world. If he's not your father, who is he then? I thought.

"Hurry," Sheriff Alexander said.

You could tell he fretted more and more about getting back across the river. I stepped out of the empty hole I'd made and started again, closer to the ash tree this time. I dug a good three feet before my shovel brought up something that wasn't a root or rock. I kneeled down and rubbed the dirt off, dirt a different shade than what I'd dug before.

It was a chain, two pieces of rusty metal dangling from it. I closed my hand around the pieces. I didn't do it hard but they crumbled like butterfly wings. I dug faster now. I found a medal with the silk still attached, a couple of boot eyelets and some bone chips. I put all of it in the sack with some of the dirt.

I kept digging but all I found was a few shards of Indian pottery and more roots.

"That's all there is, son," Sheriff Alexander said.

I didn't want to believe that. I didn't know what I thought I was going to find but it was ever so much more than what laid at the bottom of the cabbage sack.

"Let's go," Sheriff Alexander said, his hand settling firm on my shoulder, because I still kneeled on the ground, sifting through the mud for something I might have missed. But I knew I was searching for something I wasn't going to find.

I stood up and looked at the people who'd raised me. What am I supposed to do? What am I supposed to feel? I wanted to ask.

We sloshed back through the woods, my mind still tangled as memories grabbed hold of me like briars. I remembered him sitting on the bed, waiting for me to fall back asleep after a nightmare.

"You get that from me," he'd said. "I had bad dreams when I was a kid, too." He'd patted me on the shoulder. "Don't fret, son. You'll soon outgrow it same as I did."

Then another memory tore into me, a night years later at the county fair when I'd raised a pellet gun and hit the bull's eye. "You're a good aim, just like your daddy," Momma had said. His eyes had met hers and Momma's face had lost its smile and the teddy bear I gave her couldn't bring that smile back.

And the memory that tore deepest of all, because it was one that asked a question I had to answer.

"You're a Winchester, aren't you?" Mr. Pipkin had asked.

When we got to the bank the water was higher but that wasn't the worst of it. The river was muddy now. There'd be no way to tell where we stepped.

Sheriff Alexander unraveled his rope.

"You best leave those shovels," he told us. His teeth chattered as he spoke. "You're going to have enough trouble getting yourself across."

He nodded at the sack in my hand.

"You could leave that too. You could save us all a lot of trouble if you did. My deputy's on his way up here. Once he sees what's in that sack this is a murder case."

I looked at Momma and the man who'd raised me. Beg me to do what he says, I thought. Make this somehow easier. But they didn't say a word.

I knew at that moment I had to make a choice between the man who'd raised me or the sack of bones and dirt in my hand, and that choice had to be made on this side of the river. It wasn't near that simple, of course. It wasn't a matter of what was the right or the wrong thing to do or what I owed the men who claimed me as a son or to Momma or Mrs. Winchester. The only thing that mattered was what I could live with.

I stepped into the river and didn't stop until the water got to my knees. I turned, my eyes on Momma and Daddy. The current pushed hard against my legs but I stood firm. I grabbled the Gold Star from my pocket and dropped it in the sack. I raised the sack in my right hand and held it between us for a moment before I let it slip through my fingers. The current toted the sack a few feet downstream before it sunk.

"Let the dead bury the dead," Sheriff Alexander said.

Nobody else spoke or moved. For a few seconds the only sound was the rain.

Then Sheriff Alexander threw me the rope end and I started across water that seemed a lot colder than a half hour ago. I waded blind now, moving my feet slow and careful across a bottom I couldn't see. The current ran stronger, pushing me below where we'd crossed earlier. I wasn't halfway and the water almost reached my waist.

I didn't know whether to go back or go on. I just stood there, my brain working like it was in slow motion. I looked back at the others, spread out across the water with the rope in their hands like we were working a seine.

"Go on," Sheriff Alexander shouted from the shallows and I did, because I no longer seemed able to think clearly for myself.

I unraveled the rope from my hand. If I slipped I didn't want to carry them with me. I took a few more steps and the water started to get shallow again.

Suddenly the rope tightened.

"I'm caught," Daddy shouted. "My leg's in some timber."

He had one hand on his leg, the other clutching the rope. The water pressed against him and I knew he couldn't keep his balance long.

"Hold on to the rope," I shouted.

His eyes met mine. I took a step toward him, then another. I kept my eyes locked on his, almost like they were another rope to keep him up. He must have felt the same way for he didn't so much as blink. For a moment the river and rain weren't there. It was just me and him.

Then the current bent him like it would a reed and he went under. Momma went under too, jerking the rope from my hand and the Sheriff's. I lost my balance, the current carrying me into deep water where cold ran up my spine like electricity. When I came up I didn't see anyone but Momma, who was downstream.

I tried to swim back to where Daddy had gone under but the current shoved me farther downstream with every stroke. I turned and saw the back of Momma's head bobbing as the water pushed her into an eddy.

I let the water tug me downstream but the current swept me past Momma. When the current slowed I was ten yards below her. I managed to get out of the main current and into the eddy. I swam toward Momma and yelled at her to swim toward me. But the cold had numbed her brain. She looked my way but it was like she didn't even recognize me.

She turned her face upstream toward where Daddy had gone under. She raised her arms out of the water and started splashing, trying to swim toward him. Then she raised her arms above her head like she was surrendering. Her head went under and her arms and finally her hands.

"Momma!" I shouted.

I swam to where she'd gone under. I took a deep breath and dove but the current had taken her away. I dove four times, the current pushing me farther downstream until the water was no more than hip-high again. I bumped up against a big log and that gave me the leverage to stand up to the current. My teeth rattled and my mind was groggy.

Then it was like I forgot who I was looking for or even where I was. It suddenly seemed stupid to be fighting the current when I could just lay down and let it cover me like a warm blanket. I leaned back the same way I'd lean back in a bed. I felt the water cover me and for a few moments everything became dark and peaceful.

Then I felt hands on me, strong hands, pulling me back to the surface, dragging me toward shore.

"You could have let me sleep a while longer, Daddy," I said, then everything went dark again.

the DEPUTY

YOU had best get up to Billy Holcombe's place," the sheriff had said, but never a damn word about why. Which wasn't any surprise as he's always been a man stingy with his words. I finished my coffee before I put on my yellow slicker and locked up, because he hadn't said "Get here quick" or "This is serious." Hell, it could have been a damn cat up a tree for all the hurry-up in his voice.

The rain made it a slow haul up the mountain but I finally slid and spun up Billy Holcombe's drive. I saw the sheriff's car and a pick-up near the water but I wasn't about to try to drive through that field. I reckoned one stuck county vehicle was enough.

It was like slogging through a big hog pen to get to the river. Every step I had to reach down and pull my leg out of the mud like it had took root. Once my shoe came off, and I had to dig it out like it was a potato.

I shouldn't have bothered. That pair of shoes was beyond ruined before I was halfway to the water. I thought how nice it would be if I was back at the office, drinking coffee and listening to the rain hit the roof instead of being out in the midst of it. I was thinking I sure as hell hope this is something to be settled quick.

Then I saw someone coming across what had been bottomland, carrying something in his arms. I couldn't put no face on him because the rain flailed down so hard it was like looking through a waterfall. That water he came plodding through was shallow, so shallow he looked to be walking on it, like he was a haint rising from the river.

He came closer and I saw it wasn't no haint, but what he carried in his arms might well have been for the boy looked for sure more dead than alive, his face white as caulk.

"What in God's name happened?" I asked.

"What?" the sheriff said, shivering so hard he stuttered it out.

I looked into his eyes and they were damn near empty as the eyes of a jack-o'-lantern. Hypothermia and maybe shock, I was thinking.

"Come on," I said. "I got to get you and that boy thawed out."

I led him over to the car and got the both of them in the backseat.

"Get those clothes off you and him," I said, but his hands fumbled so bad he couldn't undo the first button. I did it for him, then got a blanket from the trunk and wrapped them in it. I cranked the car and got the heat going good, then called the rescue squad.

"We got us a shit-load of trouble up here," I said. I told them where I was and that they'd damn well better hurry.

I looked in the back seat. The boy was passed out cold but for his trembling, but the warmth roused the sheriff a little.

"Billy and Amy Holcombe's still down there," he said, his voice still shivery. "I got to go try and find them."

"You ain't going nowhere," I said. "You stay here with that boy and watch over him till the rescue squad gets here. I'll go find the others."

~

But I didn't find Billy and Amy Holcombe. I sent the divers down that afternoon soon as the rain slacked off. Those poor bastards had a time of it and not just because of the water being muddy. The timber the loggers left made it a rough go as well. It was easy enough for the living as well as the dead to get snagged under a mess of timber, especially in a lake where nothing had settled.

"I'll see you tomorrow," I told the divers when they gave up for the day.

The next morning I drove back up to Jocassee but I didn't head straight to Billy Holcombe's place. There was other dead I had to tend to first.

I got to the cemetery before anyone else. I looked for the divers but they still worked upstream near the Holcombe place. Every few minutes a dynamite blast near the dam shuddered the ground, blasts so loud they made my ears ring. Loud enough to raise the dead, the old people would say, but whether it would or wouldn't raise the dead didn't matter a bit. The dead was going to be raised anyway.

Melvin Pearson and his crew showed up directly, the hearse and two trucks coming slow up the road.

"How's the sheriff and the boy doing?" Melvin asked.

"They're still in the county hospital," I said, "but the doctors claim they'll both be out by tomorrow."

"Any chance the others are still alive?" Melvin asked.

"I don't see it likely," I said. "We walked both sides of the river all the way to Laurel Fork."

We watched Melvin's men pull the shovels and picks off the back of the trucks.

"It's probably for the best the sheriff's not here to see this," Melvin said.

"He'd be certain pissed-off," I said.

The sheriff had made himself no friends with his petitions and lawsuits and such. Few had felt the same way he had about not moving the graves and certainly not Carolina Power or Preacher Robertson. Or me for that matter, for my uncle was in this graveyard.

The eight men Melvin brought walked toward tin stobs with plastic name tags on them. Stobs that marked where granite and marble and soapstone had once been. The men was all gray-haired, some of them older than you would have thought to do such work, older than some of the folks they was digging up. They worked slow and deliberate as mules and spoke not a word among themselves. As the holes got deeper they stepped into the graves.

I couldn't help but wonder what it felt like to be so old and be that near death. I wondered if it made them think how close they was to their own graves. But maybe they didn't think about anything like that at all. Maybe it was just a job and meant no more to them than digging up a septic tank.

A worker in the oldest part of the cemetery stopped digging first. He didn't say a word, just nodded at Melvin.

"Excuse me," Melvin said and went and opened the back of his hearse.

Melvin lifted out what looked to be a baby casket and carried it to the grave. The old man filled it with pine knots, a silk tie and brass belt buckle, and, last, a few spadefuls of dirt. Mr. Pearson closed the lid and wrote something on the wood before he laid it in the truck bed.

Another worker soon raised his hand, this time from the section of the graveyard where my uncle was buried. But it wasn't my uncle he'd found. It was Sheriff Alexander's daddy.

There was a coffin this time. The workers tried to be careful, but the wood was so rotten the bottom gave way and the skeleton shattered like it was made of matchsticks.

Yes, it's a hell of a good thing the sheriff ain't here, I thought.

I reckoned something else as well, that maybe he was the only one who'd had any real notion what this was going to be like. I was coming around to his way of thinking real fast.

"This is wrong, Melvin," I said as workers picked up pieces of the sheriff's daddy no bigger than chinquapins.

"We're doing the best we can," Melvin said, sulling up on me a bit. "This ain't no easy job. We'll have them Christian buried by afternoon. Preacher Robertson's going to say a prayer and bless that ground and everybody put in it."

I looked out toward the river for I reckoned you could call it a river for a while longer at least. I saw that the divers had worked their way downstream near the church. Of a sudden I had a thought of months more passing, that church underwater and divers still hunting for Billy and Amy Holcombe. I imagined divers swimming around inside, moving above the pews and pulpit like angels, morning sun streaming through the water and church-window glass making pretty colors all about them.

It was a nice enough picture I painted in my head. But it was a damn lie. Those divers in their black wet suits would be like buzzards if they was like anything as they made slow circles above the pulpit and pews, their eyes looking down to spot something dead.

"My own momma was in that other cemetery we moved, Bobby," Melvin said, pulling my eyes and thoughts from the church. "I've done no worse here than I've done to my own beloved."

I nodded. Melvin was just doing his job, doing it as best he could. It wasn't a particularly agreeable job, but mine wasn't either at times. I reckoned we were both in the same shitty business of dealing with other people's bad news.

One of the workers moved to my Uncle Luke's grave. I didn't want to see what he was now. I wanted to remember the way I'd seen him last, laid out in his front room for the wake. He hadn't looked good then but at least he'd looked like a human being.

"I got to go check on the divers," I told Melvin. "Send one of your men if you need me."

"I'll do that, Bobby," he said.

I walked out the gate to my car. I could still hear the shovelfuls of dirt hit the ground, the raspy sound the shovels made as they broke into the earth.

~

"Give it a couple of weeks," the county coroner Calvin Rochester said when the divers gave up after three days. "There's a good chance they'll rise on their own."

But for the next six months the only thing that rose was the water, covering up houses and barns and roads, turning creeks into coves, sinking Billy and Amy Holcombe deeper and deeper.

It was spring when a body finally did come up, but it wasn't one folks had been searching for. This body already had been buried.

One of Carolina Power's people found a coffin bobbing in the middle of the lake like some fisherman's trotline, so they called the sheriff and Calvin.

"You go take care of it," the sheriff said to me.

When I got there they had the coffin hid in a shed with a guard out front to make sure nobody came snooping around. They was smart enough to know if word got out about such a thing people in Oconee County would be stirred up like hornets. The Carolina Power man said as much to me and Calvin, asking us not to say nothing to anyone about what he called a "unfortunate occurrence."

"We've spoken to Pearson Funeral Home," he told us. "As soon as you men give the O.K., they'll get it in the ground with the others they dug up."

"That shouldn't be a problem," Calvin said. "This won't take but a minute."

The Carolina Power man lifted the tarp off the coffin. I didn't have to see any more than the wood to know what was inside.

Calvin gave the body a quick look-see and laid the coffin lid back on.

"O.K," Calvin said. "You tell Melvin Pearson he can rebury it. You got any problem with that, Bobby?"

"No," I said. "But it's best I be the one to deliver it."

Calvin looked a little puzzled.

"That's what the sheriff would want you to do?" Calvin asked.

"Yes," I said.

Calvin shrugged his shoulders.

"Well, I guess that's fine by me," he said.

The Carolina Power man didn't say nothing either way. He was just happy as hell to get that coffin off his hands. They helped me load it in the back seat, one end poking out the window like I was hauling a piece of furniture.

"Please tell Mr. Pearson we'd like him to get it reburied today if at all possible," the Carolina Power man said.

"I'll tell him," I said.

I started toward Seneca but when I got to Highway 11, I took a right toward Mountain Rest. The largemouth bass was spawning, and my brother might have quit early and took the boat out himself. That was my worry, for I'd be in a tangle if that was the way of it. But when I drove up Wendell's drive the jon boat was beside the barn.

Wendell was working in his corn field. When he saw me drive up he hopped off his tractor and walked out of his field to meet me.

"I need your boat," I said. "Your truck too, I reckon, since I got no hitch."

"That ain't no problem," he said. "The rain's put me so behind I'll be lucky if I wet a line by August."

Wendell went inside the barn and got the motor.

"Let's get it hooked up," he said.

He backed up the truck while I lifted the trailer hitch.

"There," he said, handing me the keys after we got the motor on. "Make sure you give that cord a few yanks for it's stubborn to start."

Wendell looked ready to get back in his corn field but I nodded toward the police car.

"If you got a minute I could use another set of hands."

We lifted the coffin and laid it in the boat. I got a blanket and rope out of the trunk and covered it.

"Damn, Bobby," Wendell said when we'd finished. "What are you about to be up to?"

"It wouldn't do you a speck of good to know," I said. "But if you was to know you'd be glad I was doing it."

He mulled that over a few moments. You could tell he was curious as a cat about that coffin.

"Anything else you need?" Wendell asked.

"Just a box of salt."

Twenty minutes later I left the blacktop and bumped down what was already being called Old Jocassee Road. I parked where the road disappeared into the water. I got the boat in and headed toward the heart of the lake.

I drove slow, for the coffin made it a damn awkward balance. The jon boat rode high, though if that coffin had been oak instead of cedar it would have been a hell of a different story. Carolina Power claimed there'd be places four hundred foot deep when the lake filled up completely. When I got to where I figured one might would be, I cut the engine.

"Still waters run deep," my Grandma Murphree used to say, "and the devil lays at the bottom."

I lifted the blanket and lid. I looked in the coffin and saw her old hollow-eyed skull grinning at me.

"You'll not rest in no graveyard with my kin, witch," I told her. Then I lifted what there was of her from the coffin.

"Sink straight to hell," I said and dropped her in the water.

The clearest water of any lake in the South—that was another Carolina Power claim, and I could believe it. I watched those bones drift down, the skull-face nodding back and forth, the arms unfolding off her ribs and spreading out like wings, getting smaller and smaller, the lake so clear it was like she fell through air, not water.

When I couldn't see her no more I yanked the cord and headed back. It was a blue-sky afternoon, the kind of warm, perfect day you sometimes get around here in spring, the kind of day to get out on water like this with a rod and reel and give yourself a chance to leave your bothers behind and be trifling a few hours.

You got done what you had to do, I told myself. Just relax now and enjoy the scenery and let your mind drift. But I couldn't because my mind kept snagging on Billy and Amy Holcombe. Which wasn't the least surprising thing considering where I was. I was thinking how they was dead and sunk in the lake and wasn't going to rise till the Judgment Day.

I thought about their son too. How he was living with the sheriff until he went down to Clemson in the fall. I wondered if he'd be like the sheriff and never come back up here, even to grieve.

I was getting near shore now so I eased the throttle. I looked at the bank and realized I was eyeballing the top of Licklog Mountain. Down in the water I saw a road and I knew there was but one road it could be. Everything was so clear it was like looking through a window. I cut the engine and let the boat drift above the old river bed, the boat's shadow dragging across the lake bottom like a net.

This is the way God sees the world, I thought. Soon I saw the truck, still bogged down in the mud the way it had been six months ago, then a mailbox and finally the house and barn and shed me and the sheriff had searched so long ago.

The front door of the house was open and I couldn't shake the feeling that someone might step out on that porch any second and look up at me the same way I might look up at a plane—someone who didn't even know they was dead and buried under a lake.

That thought sent a hell of a shiver up my spine. I didn't want to be on this water no more. I yanked the cord and got to shore quick as I could. I hitched the jon boat to the trailer and drove up the road a few yards. I lifted the coffin lid and spread the salt around the inside, then threw in some rocks before I closed it. When I got back to Wendell's I'd hammer a few nails in the lid just in case Melvin or one of his workers took a notion to peek inside.

I drove out of Jocassee, for the last time if I had any say in the matter. I wouldn't be coming back here to fish or water ski or swim or anything else like that. This wasn't no place for people who had a home.

This was a place for the lost.